"You know what they say about the way to a man's heart."

She stiffened visibly, and Carter wanted to rope the words he'd just spoken and yank them back into his mouth.

"I should get going," she said, pulling her van keys from the purse slung over her shoulder.

"Audra," he said apologetically, knowing she wasn't looking to be part of any man's heart. She'd made that pretty clear. Friendship was as far as anything could ever go between them. But he found himself wanting more. He chose his next words carefully.

"I know what you've gone through and understand your need to be guarded. But the truth is, I'd like to move beyond a working relationship where you're concerned."

"Carter," she said in a panicked whisper, "please don't."

"Friendship, Audra," he said determinedly. "That's all I'm asking for. Like you, I'm not looking for anything more right now," he added, hoping it would ease her worry. It wasn't a lie. He knew that there would be no "right now" with her.

But tomorrow, or the day after… Well, that was another story.

Kat Brookes is an award-winning author and past Romance Writers of America Golden Heart® Award finalist. She is married to her childhood sweetheart and has been blessed with two beautiful daughters. She loves writing stories that can both make you smile and touch your heart. Kat is represented by Michelle Grajkowski with 3 Seas Literary Agency. Read more about Kat and her upcoming releases at katbrookes.com. Email her at katbrookes@comcast.net. Facebook: Kat Brookes.

Books by Kat Brookes

Love Inspired

Texas Sweethearts

Her Texas Hero

Her Texas Hero

Kat Brookes

HARLEQUIN® LOVE INSPIRED®

Recycling programs for this product may not exist in your area.

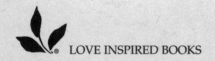

LOVE INSPIRED BOOKS

ISBN-13: 978-0-373-81935-5

Her Texas Hero

Copyright © 2016 by Kimberly Duffy

www.Harlequin.com

Printed in U.S.A.

For if you forgive others their trespasses,
your heavenly Father will also forgive you.
—*Matthew* 6:14

To my husband, whom I adore. You are my heart. Thank you for your never-ending love and support, and for showing me that real heroes can be found beyond the pages of fiction.

Chapter One

Carter Cooper grabbed for the ringing cell phone on the truck seat beside him. A quick glance at the screen listed Nathan Cooper as the caller. Swiping his thumb over the answer button, he brought the phone to his ear.

"Missing me already, big brother?"

Nathan snorted. "Hardly. But I am missing the keys to my truck. You got any idea where they might have gotten to?"

A smile quirked at the corners of Carter's mouth. "Can you describe them to me? Might help jog my memory some."

"Carter," Nathan growled impatiently.

"What's wrong, Nate? You can dish it out, but you can't take it?" His brother and business partner in Cooper Construction had thought it funny to line the back of Carter's safety goggles with black shoe polish. Carter glanced up in the rearview mirror where, beneath the mirrored lenses of his sunglasses, the remainder of what he hadn't been able to scrub off at the job site remained.

"It was Logan's idea," his brother grumbled.

"And you executed it." Their younger brother, Logan, was the real prankster of the family, but he was good at getting others to join in. Or in this instance, pull off the prank for him. The fact that his little brother had gotten Nathan to play along was worth the thick black smudging he was sporting around his eyes. After losing their parents, along with his older brother's wife, in the tornado that had ripped through their tiny town of Braxton more than a year ago, Nathan seemed to have lost himself, as well. He knew the only thing that kept his big brother from giving up on life, at least as far as Carter was concerned, was Nathan's beautiful little daughter, Katie. Or as Carter was fond of calling his six-year-old niece—Katydid.

"All right, guilty as charged," his brother conceded. "Now where are my truck keys?"

"You know that bucket of wall primer…?" Carter teased as he turned off the main road, intending to take a shortcut into town, where he would swing by the hardware store and pick up something to take the remaining shoe polish off his face.

His brother groaned. "Tell me you didn't."

"I didn't," Carter said with a chuckle. "They're…" His words trailed off as his attention was drawn to movement outside the open driver's side window. Just past the wildly overgrown hedgerow that lined the inside of the faded white property fence, a woman lay facedown atop the sagging porch roof of the old abandoned Harris house. At least, the upper half of her did. The rest of her dangled down over the roof's edge.

Slowing his truck, he glanced back at the scene he'd just driven by. Crime was virtually nonexistent in Braxton, Texas. And the only thing anyone would find in that old place would be cobwebs and dust balls, so he immediately wrote off the possibility of a robbery. So what was that woman doing up on the old farmhouse's porch roof?

That last thought had barely surfaced when a high-pitched cry cut through the warm spring air. "Help!"

"Carter?" his brother prompted, his impatience growing.

"In the toolbox," he blurted out. "Gotta go." He disconnected the call, then stepped on the brake. Throwing his truck into Reverse, he backed up to the drive that led to the dilapidated old farmhouse that no one had lived in for a good ten years or more.

Sure enough, the woman dangled from the edge of the aging farmhouse's sagging porch roof. She was definitely in trouble. Carter turned his truck into the dirt-and-gravel drive and drove at breakneck speed up to the house, sending a billowing cloud of dust up into the air behind him.

He was out of the truck in no time, racing toward the wraparound porch where the wooden ladder the woman had been using to climb onto the roof had kicked away and was now resting haphazardly against the thick, sprawling branch of a honey mesquite.

The woman was fortunate, he thought with a concerned frown. If the tree hadn't taken root so close to the old farmhouse… Well, he wasn't even going to think about what the outcome might have been. As it was, one flip-flop-covered foot rested at an awkward angle against the top rung of the rickety old ladder. The woman's other foot, currently shoeless, struggled to find purchase below her with no success.

"Hold on!" he called out to her. And then he did something he hadn't done since his daddy and poor little Katie had been taken to the hospital after the tornado. He prayed.

Lord, please let me reach this woman in time.

Years of working construction, much of that time spent atop ladders, told him that her legs wouldn't be able to hold out for long before cramping would set in.

"Mommy!" a tiny voice whimpered.

Carter's gaze shot up to the second-story window just beyond the woman, noticing for the first time the two little faces peeking out, eyes wide with worry.

"Mommy's fine, sweetie," she replied, her words strained. "I've got a hold on the rope loop Mason made for me."

His gaze shifted to the length of what looked to be a half-inch manila rope that spilled out over the open windowsill and ran down the weathered asphalt shingles. At the end of the rope was a large loop, which the woman held in a determinedly white-knuckled grasp.

He stepped up to the fallen ladder, just beneath her dangling form. "Are you injured?"

"No," she called down. "But I seem to have lost my other flip-flop."

She could have lost a lot more than that, he thought, his frown deepening. "It's right here on the ground," he told her as he eyed the cotton-candy-pink flip-flop lying on the grass in front of a flowering Texas sage shrub. "What are you doing up there anyway?" he called up to her with a frown.

"Retrieving a Frisbee."

His dark brow shot up. *A Frisbee?* The woman had risked her neck for a Frisbee? "How about we rescue you instead?"

"I…I'm okay with that."

His mouth quirked, despite the seriousness of the situation. "I'm gonna reposition this ladder, but I want you to keep your foot braced against it while I do. Then I'm gonna hold the ladder in place so you can climb down."

"Sounds like a plan," she said unevenly.

He couldn't see her face from where he stood, but he didn't have to see it to know she was more shaken than she was letting on. "Okay, I'm gonna start lifting the ladder back toward the roof." He raised it slow enough to allow the woman to maintain her foothold, prepared to catch her if her foot slipped and she fell. "Okay, work your other foot over to the ladder," he told her the moment he had the ladder firmly back in place.

Ever so tentatively, her bare foot felt its way to the top rung. Her long ponytail swung ever so slightly behind her, the afternoon sun bringing out the glints of gold in the honey-brown strands.

"That's it, darlin'," he said, his grip firm on the ladder.

Her legs trembled beneath her, making the

ladder vibrate. The shudder was subtle, but it told him that her strength was nearly spent. "Steady…" he said, wishing he could go up to get her. But the ladder was old and too unsteady to risk it. No, he had to make this work. In doing so, he offered up another silent prayer for the Lord to deliver her safely to the ground below.

"Now work your way down," he coaxed calmly.

She started to step down and then stopped. "I can't. The rope isn't long enough."

He glanced up toward the window. "What's that rope secured to anyway?"

"An old iron bed," she replied shakily. "At least, the frame. There's no mattress. It's the only thing in the room."

"If that bed frame's in the same shape as that roof you're lying on and this ladder I'm holding on to, it's best we don't have you holding on to that rope much longer. You're gonna have to let go of it so you can grab on to the ladder."

"What if I fall?" she said, sounding on the verge of tears. "I can't fall. My children need me. I'm all they have."

He thought of the two frightened faces he saw in the window above. Her children were counting on him to get their momma down safely. A feeling like he'd never known came over him and he knew that God had turned him down her road, one he rarely ever traveled on, for a reason.

"I'm not gonna let you fall," he assured her.

"And if I do?" she demanded with a muffled sob.

"I'll catch you," he answered without hesitation. "Either way, you're safe with me."

You're safe with me. Audra Marshall replayed those words over and over in her mind as she moved down the old ladder. They were the same words she'd heard before from the man who'd promised to love her forever. A man who'd failed to hold to his vows, leaving her to raise their two young children alone.

"Mommy?" her nearly five-year-old daughter called down worriedly. "Are you going to leave us, too?"

"Mommy's not going anywhere," she quickly assured her little girl, having heard the panic in her voice. Then she felt herself being lifted from the ladder into a pair of strong arms. "I'm…" She'd almost said she was safe now, but considering she was being held in the arms of a man she didn't know, she couldn't bring herself to say those words. She did, however, say a prayer of thanks to God for watching over her. Not that she'd expected the help she'd prayed for, while clinging frantically to the loop of rope her son had tossed down to her, to show up in the form of a Texas cowboy. Hat and all.

"Why don't you kids pull that rope back in through the window and untie it? Then bring it on down with you?" the man hollered up toward the roof's overhang. Then he muttered, "The last thing we need is for one of them to use that rope to climb out onto the roof to see that you're all right."

"I've raised my children to have more sense than that," she said stiffly, automatically defensive when it came to even the slightest criticism where her son and daughter were concerned. Her ex-husband had done nothing but that for the past three years.

The man holding her securely in his strong arms paused midstep to look down at her from behind the mirrored shades of his sunglasses, which were shadowed by the brim of his cowboy hat. Then his head tilted ever so slightly upward, and if she had her guess she'd say he'd just rolled his eyes heavenward beneath the concealing lenses of his sunglasses.

"I would hope they do," he said. "But I did just save their momma from breaking her pretty little neck after she tried to retrieve a plastic disc from a rotted roof using a ladder better used for kindling than climbing on."

"I didn't know the roof was rotted," she replied with a frown. "Just a little sunken." The ladder, however, she had actually hesitated in using. But after a moment's indecision, she'd given in, deciding that it looked strong enough to hold her for the short time it would take for her to grab her son's Frisbee and toss it down. What she hadn't counted on was having it tip out from under her.

"Maybe so," he said, "but I'm not about to risk your little ones getting hurt because they don't know better, either."

She looked up at him in stunned surprise. Here was a man who didn't even know her children, yet he was voicing his concern, rather adamantly, about their well-being, when their own father couldn't care less. She couldn't keep the tears from filling her eyes.

"Ma'am," he said, his deep, baritone voice laced with concern. "Are you hurt?"

She fought back the tears, shaking her head. "No, I...I'm fine. Just a little shaken." And sore. Every muscle in her body felt like she'd just rolled down a steep hillside. "I appreciate your concern for my children. I'll have a talk with them and make certain they know never to go out onto that roof. Any roof for that matter."

He nodded. "Glad to hear it. Now let's get you over to that porch swing," he said as he headed for the crumbling walkway that led to the old farmhouse's deep-set porch.

"I can walk," she protested without much conviction as she clung to her rescuer's wide shoulders. Despite her stubborn determination to stand on her own two feet, she honestly wasn't sure she could at that moment. She felt like a rag doll without any stuffing.

"Humor me," he replied, his long strides never slowing until he had her lowered safely onto the porch swing, which, thankfully, appeared to be sturdier than the ladder she had found in the garage.

"Thank you for coming to my rescue, Mr...."

"Cooper," he said as he took a step back, putting some distance between them. "Carter Cooper."

"Audra Marshall," she replied with a tentative smile as she settled back against the swing, her legs trembling. Her right calf ached from having been perched on the ball of her foot atop the ladder rung for so long. She attempted to stretch the cramping limb, pointing her toes downward. Before she could lift her toes upward to complete the motion, the muscle in her calf knotted up painfully, drawing a soft cry from her lips.

Vivid blue eyes studied her. "Cramp?" Carter Cooper asked worriedly.

"Yes," she gasped as tears once again filled her eyes.

Kneeling in front of her, he lifted her foot, flip-flop and all, in his large hand and then gently pushed her toes upward, effectively stretching the contracting muscle.

"What are you doing?" Her words came out in a pained whisper.

He looked up at her from beneath the brim of his cowboy hat. "Working the cramp out," he said matter-of-factly. Then his focus returned to the painfully knotted muscle in her leg. Keeping the pressure steady, he held her foot in place for several seconds before easing up on the tension he'd been applying. Then he repeated the motion once more. "Helping?"

"Yes," she said, pulling her leg free of his grasp. "It seems I'm indebted to you yet again."

Looking up at her, he said, "I only did what my momma raised me to do."

"Please thank your mother for me," she said with a smile. "She raised a very thoughtful son."

His mouth pulled into a grimace. Then he straightened to tower over her. "Afraid I can't do that," he said. "We lost her two Christmases ago."

"I'm so sorry to hear that," she said, her heart going out to him. She'd lost both her parents in a boating accident on Lake Michigan the summer after her high school graduation. Maybe if that hadn't happened she wouldn't have rushed into marriage, needing to fill the void her parents' death had left in her life. No, she probably would have married Bradford anyway. Several years older than her, he'd been a good Christian man with a financially stable job who said all the right things. Sent her flowers. She'd loved him and she thought he'd loved her back. And maybe he had. Until the children were born and he was no longer the sole focus of her attention.

"If your leg starts cramping up again," her rescuer began, that deep, husky voice pulling her from her troubled musings, "there are a couple of things you can do to try and relieve it. Massage your calf to work the cramp out, or stretch it out like I just did, holding it for a few seconds. Then ease up, repeating the motion until you feel the muscle relax. A warm shower can help as well."

"Thank you," she said. "I'll keep your suggestions in mind."

He nodded and had just reached up to remove his sunglasses, which were unnecessary now that he was standing beneath the cooling shade of the porch, when the screen door flung open with a loud groan, drawing his attention that way. A second later, her son and daughter flew out of the house.

"Mommy!" four-year-old Lily cried out, racing toward Audra with her tiny arms outstretched, bypassing the towering cowboy without even a moment's hesitation in her eagerness to reach her.

"Mo—" her son began and then stopped with a gasp halfway across the porch. Green eyes widening, Mason, coiled rope in hand, stood staring up at her rescuer, who was well over six feet in height. A good bit taller than what they were used to, Bradford being only five-nine on a good day.

Sunglasses dangling at his side, Carter Cooper smiled down at her son. "You must be Mason. Nice work with that rope loop."

"It's you!" her son said in what sounded like awe, still openly staring up at the man.

"Mason, honey?" she said, attempting to draw her son's attention away from their unexpected, but very much appreciated, visitor. A man the Lord had sent in answer to her fervent prayers as she'd hung, fearful for her life, from the sagging roof.

Her son's gaze finally shifted, meeting hers. "Mommy," he said excitedly, "you were rescued by the Lone Ranger!"

"The Lone Ranger?" Carter Cooper replied

with a husky chuckle. "Afraid not, son. The only thing that fictional Texas Ranger and I have in common is that we both wear cowboy hats. Unless you count the fact that I drive a *silver* Ford F-150 and the Lone Ranger rides a horse named Silver." He glanced back at Audra with a crooked grin. "My brothers would have a field day with this one."

"Sweetie, Mr. Cooper is not…" Her words trailed off as her gaze shifted from her son to her rescuer. Her hand flew to her mouth in an attempt to muffle the snort of laughter that shot through her lips as she eyed the smudging of black around his eyes that had previously been covered up by his sunglasses.

"He is the Lone Ranger!" her daughter exclaimed. "He has dark hair and he's wearing a mask," she added, pointing to the mask of black encircling his blue eyes.

"Honey, it's not polite to point," Audra said, fighting the smile that threatened to spill across her face. "But I think you're right."

The man looked from her and Lily to her son in confusion. And then his expression changed. With a groan, he pointed to the dark circles around his eyes and said, "He's referring to this?"

Audra nodded.

"It's not polite to point," her daughter told

him, mimicking her mother's earlier repri-manding words.

"It doesn't count if you're pointing your finger at yourself," Mason told his sister.

"But if he's not the Lone Ranger, why is he wearing a mask?" her daughter asked in confusion.

Audra had to admit she was wondering that same thing herself. "Can you tell they watch a lot of old Westerns?" she said lightly, trying to cover the fact she felt a little unnerved by the sight of a man who went around with his face painted like a raccoon's.

"It's all right," he assured her with a grin as he slipped the sunglasses back onto his face. "I'm wearing this *mask* because my brothers thought it would be funny to play a prank on me."

"Your brothers did that to you?" she said, unable to hide the relief that flooded her voice. Being new to Braxton, Texas, she knew nothing about the people who lived there. She only knew that the tiny town had rated well when it came to crime of any kind. A true safe haven to raise her children in. And it was in Texas, a place she and the children had been drawn to thanks to all those old Westerns they loved to watch together on TV.

He nodded. "Their idea of a joke."

She fought to keep the grin from her face, not wanting to be impolite at his expense. "How naughty of them."

"How did they do it?" her son asked with that same uncontainable curiosity most boys his age were filled with. "Did they pin you to the ground and paint your face?"

"Are you going to paint me?" Lily asked her brother, a worried look on her tiny face.

"No," Audra said. "Your brother is not going to paint you."

"How they did it isn't important," Carter Cooper replied. "They've since realized the error of their ways. At least, my older brother has. I haven't seen my younger brother yet to set him straight." He looked around and then back at her. "I should get going. I was on my way into town to pick up something to get this off my face when I noticed you hanging from the roof."

The sooner he was on his way, the better, Audra thought. While she was grateful to the man for coming to her rescue, she didn't want her children's fascination with Carter Cooper to grow any more than it was at that moment, with their having thought him to be one of their favorite TV characters come to life. Or even worse, their becoming attached to him in any way whatsoever. She wouldn't allow that to happen. Couldn't allow it to happen. Not when her children had already been forced to deal with their father turning his back on them. Whatever it took, she would protect their young hearts from feeling the pain of abandonment ever again.

"I'd offer to help you remove it," she said, knowing it was the least she could have done after what he'd done for her, "but we only just arrived and almost everything we own is still packed in boxes in my van and in the moving truck that's on its way. I wanted to check things out and give the children a chance to play outside a bit before we started moving in."

His dark brow shot up. "You bought this place?"

She nodded. "Through an online auction site."

He glanced around, his mouth pulling down into a frown.

She completely understood his reaction, having seen the place now for herself. "I have to admit it looked a little more promising in pictures."

His gaze shifted back to her. "Are you telling me you purchased this house after seeing it only in pictures online?"

She looked down at her daughter, running her fingers through Lily's tangled golden-brown curls. "Traveling from Illinois to Texas and back just to see a house that was advertised as being in need of some tender loving care seemed like a waste of money that could be used on those repairs instead."

"Not to be the bearer of bad news," he said with a frown, "but this place is in need of far more than some tender loving care. If the inside is anything like the outside, you're looking at a near total gut, if not a complete one."

A total gut? Surely he was exaggerating. She glanced around with a troubled frown. "I think it looks worse than it is." At least, she hoped so. She couldn't afford to totally renovate the whole house inside and out. Not with Bradford still owing her court-ordered child support for the time he was still considered legally their father. At least she had her half of the money from the sale of their house in Chicago, minus the few months' rent she'd had to pay while looking for a place for her and her children to start their lives again.

"My curtains are made of spiderwebs," Lily announced, scrunching up her tiny nose.

"And the back door won't open," Mason added with a frown.

Embarrassment warmed Audra's cheeks. "Cobwebs can be swept away and the door just needs a little oil."

The man cleared his throat. "I doubt oiling the door is gonna fix your problem. Chances are the door is a little swollen from all the rain and humidity we've had in the past few weeks." He glanced around. "As old as this place is and knowing how long it's been sitting here unattended to, there's a real good possibility the foundation has shifted and it's throwing things off."

The foundation? That sounded more than a little costly. "You sound like you've dealt with this problem before," she said, wondering how he could know these things when he hadn't even taken a look at her door yet. Maybe this was a common problem in Texas.

"I have," he replied with a nod. "My brother and I own a construction company. We do a lot of home renovations as well as new builds. I'd be happy to take a look at your door and give you an idea of what you'll need to do to fix the problem."

"Maybe Daddy could fix it," Lily suggested.

Audra cringed at her daughter's hopeful words.

"We don't have a daddy anymore," Mason reminded her in a tone laced with both hurt and anger.

"I forgot," Lily said woefully. Then, looking

up at a sober-faced Carter Cooper, she added, "Our daddy gave us away."

Before Audra had a chance to respond, her son puffed out his chest and announced, "I'm the man of the house now."

Guilt weighed heavily on her heart. "My husband and I are divorced," she said, somehow managing to get the words past the emotion constricting her throat. "He decided fatherhood wasn't for him and gave up his parental rights." Her bottom lip quivered as she fought the urge to cry. Maybe it was the long drive to Texas, or even the scare she'd had up on the roof, but her emotions felt incredibly raw at that moment.

She had failed as a wife and now as a mother if one listened to her children's words. At six years old, her son shouldn't have to be the "man of the house." And no child should ever feel like their father simply gave them away. But everything they said was true. Mason was the only male in the house and their father had signed over all rights to his children without even a moment's hesitation. And she had failed God, because she had spoken vows to love, honor and cherish. None of which she'd been able to bring herself to do at the end of her marriage.

But this was her chance to start over. To give her children the kind of life they deserved. One where they would feel happy and safe, never

doubting her love for them. Her gaze shifted
to the peeling porch paint and the weathered
cracks in the wood framing the porch windows
and she knew she had her work cut out for her.
But with determination, hard work and a fair
amount of prayer, she would turn this dilapidated old house into a true home for herself
and her children.

Chapter Two

Carter shifted uneasily. What did he say to that? He hated the sorrow he'd heard in Audra Marshall's voice. A woman alone, raising two young children all by herself. And now she had to deal with this dilapidated old house she'd purchased online.

Her daughter's heart-wrenching words played through his mind. *Our daddy gave us away.* What kind of man gave up his own children? Not him. At least, he wouldn't if he were ever to have a child of his own, which he had no intention of doing. He was plenty content to spoil Katie rotten and then send her home to her daddy. To think Audra's ex had so little appreciation of his beautiful little girl and smart-as-a-whip little boy made his heart ache for them.

Life was too precious. He'd learned that a little over a year before, when the F4 twister took the lives of his parents and his sister-in-law. It was a day that would never be erased from his mind. He and Nathan had been the ones to find their parents. They'd pulled their momma's lifeless body from the rubble that had once been their family home and then found their daddy, broken and bloodied, close by. By then rescuers had arrived and a desperate search went on for Isabel and Katie. Carter had been the one to find Isabel, who'd looked like a broken doll. Her last words had been "Keep them safe and happy for me, Carter." Words he would honor. Words he had kept to himself, not wanting Nathan to know his beloved wife had suffered even in the slightest before passing. It was better that way.

Katie, who the rescuers had found cut and bleeding, her leg severely broken, in what had once been his parents' hall closet, had been the only survivor. Their daddy, who had been severely injured, was called home to the Lord just a day after losing his beloved wife of thirty-two years. His brother had done his best to fill the void Isabel's death had left in their young daughter's life, but it had taken a toll on Nathan emotionally. On all of them, truth be told. The tragedy of that day had changed all of their lives forever. And unlike houses, which could be repaired, hearts were a whole different story. His brothers were living proof of that.

"You're really tall," Lily said, drawing Carter back from his troubled thoughts. She looked up at him from her perch atop the porch swing, where she sat beside her mother. The same light brown eyes flecked with gold as her mother's. The same honey-brown hair.

"Reckon I am," he replied with a grin.

"Bet you could reach the spiderweb curtains on my windows."

"Lily," Audra gasped, "Mr. Cooper is not cleaning the cobwebs from your windows."

"I happen to be real good at removing cobwebs from high places," he said. "I'd be happy to—"

"We've held Mr. Cooper up long enough," she said, not giving him the chance to offer any more assistance than he already had. Easing her young daughter upright in the swing, Audra Marshall pushed to her feet. "I'll show you to the back door so you can take a quick look at it and then you can get on your way."

As he followed her into the house, he couldn't help but wonder if she was anxious to get rid of him because he'd overstayed his welcome, or if she really felt like she'd imposed on his time.

"I'd ask you to forgive the mess," she called back over her shoulder as she made her way toward the back of the house, "but I assume you understand."

"Completely," he replied. He did a mental sweep around him. The outside was in need of major repairs, but the inside was far worse. A major undertaking for even a professional like himself. "So you're gonna be hiring someone to do the necessary repairs to the house?"

"I hadn't planned on it," she replied as she led him down a wide hallway.

"Excuse me?"

"I came here with the intention of doing most of it myself," she explained without slowing her steps.

"Mommy can fix anything," Lily said as she scurried to walk beside him. "She fixed my dolly's broken arm."

He chuckled, slowing his step to allow her to keep up. His gaze dropped down to her adorable little face. "Did she now?"

"A little glue goes a long way," Audra said, her determined strides taking her into the kitchen.

Maybe when it came to small fix-its. But glue wasn't going to make this house habitable. "You really should reconsider hiring someone on to help with the repairs."

"There are plenty of books on doing home repairs." She crossed the room and stopped next to what could only be the inoperable door. Then she turned to face him. "I'm a fast learner."

He should have known that, as determinedly as she'd hung on to keep from falling off that roof, the woman was bound to have a stubborn side. Carter stepped up to the door to inspect it. "Before I leave, I'll get that Frisbee down off the roof for you."

"I'd rather you not risk getting hurt trying to do that for us," she said with a frown.

His gaze shifted to her children, who were taking in every word like little sponges. "While I appreciate your concern for my safety," he said as he once again removed his sunglasses and shoved them down into the front pocket of his shirt, "I go up onto roofs, good ones and bad ones, for a living." He knelt to check out the doorknob and its locking mechanism. "And I'd never forgive myself for driving off with that Frisbee still up there. Too tempting for certain persons who might be stirred to try and find some way to get it off all by themselves." He gave a slight nod in the direction of the children. "That should be left to someone who knows what they're doing up on that roof."

She glanced in her children's direction. "Mr. Cooper's right. Never go up on the roof. It's too dangerous." Her gaze shifted back to him. "If you're sure you have the time to spare, I'd appreciate your help in getting it down."

"Finished up work early today," he told her, his focus returning to the stubborn old door, which was determined not to budge from the frame it was nestled far too snugly in. "Nothing else planned for the rest of my day except removing this ridiculous raccoon mask I'm sporting."

A soft giggle sounded beside him, drawing his gaze upward. He quirked a brow.

"Sorry," Audra said, not bothering to hide her amusement. "Actually," she said, studying his face more closely, "in some strange way, the 'mask' suits you."

"I'm not sure if I should thank you for the slightly offhanded compliment, or if I should put my sunglasses back on, which I will tell you will make it pretty hard to see what I'm doing here," he added, motioning toward the door.

"Compliment," she said with a smile. "Without a doubt."

She was sweet, but he didn't believe a word of her flattery. There was no doubt in his mind that he looked ridiculous. It was no wonder she wasn't jumping at the chance to hire him on for her house renovations. Who in their right mind would consider hiring on a man wearing a shoe-polish mask? He stood, straightening to his full height. "As I suspected, the door's rotted and swollen. It's gonna need to be replaced."

Her smile faded for the briefest of moments before she drew back her shoulders and lifted her chin. "We'll just have to make do with one door for a while."

One door? What if there were a fire and the front door wasn't accessible? "It could be shaved down some as a temporary fix," he suggested. "But you really should consider replacing it."

She bit her bottom lip as if mentally assessing her choices. Then she turned to her children. "Kids, run out to the van and get Mr. Cooper a bottle of water from the cooler."

Before he could tell her not to bother, her children were gone.

She turned back to him, craning her neck as she looked up at him. He hadn't realized before what a tiny thing she was. Five-three if she were fortunate. Nearly a foot shorter than his own six foot two inches. "My children have had enough to deal with in their lives. The last thing they need to do is worry about my being able to take care of them. The truth is, my funds are limited right now. So a new door is out of the question. My money needs to go to the more demanding repairs."

He nodded. That didn't mean he liked the thought of her trying to handle this project on her own. Pulling out his wallet, he withdrew his business card and handed it to her. "Since you don't know me from Adam, here's my card to prove I have a little bit of experience with these sorts of things." He wanted her to trust him. Why it mattered so much he had no idea, but it did.

She took the offered card, her gaze drifting over it. "As I've already said, hiring on a professional isn't in the budget. But with the good Lord's help we'll figure it out."

He fought the urge to frown. The good Lord might be watching over them, but home renovations were not something he'd be seeing to. And even with God's guidance Audra Marshall would not be able to do this on her own. "I'll stop by tomorrow to repair the back door."

"That won't be necessary," she said without hesitation. "Just tell me what I need to do and I'll do it."

Stubborn. Determined. Prideful female. Carter mentally ticked off a list of appropriate descriptions for Audra Marshall while he came to terms with her refusal of his offer. But it was her house. Her door. Her decision to make. So he grudgingly explained what she would have to do to fix the door. At least temporarily. "If there's anything else I can do to help," he told her, "just give me a ring. My cell phone number's on the bottom of the card."

She glanced down at the light gray business card she still clutched in her hand and then back up at him. "Thank you, but I'm sure it won't be necessary." She held out her hand, intending to give the card back to him.

"Keep it," he insisted and then added with a tempered smile, "Just in case."

He waited, fully expecting her to refuse him again. Instead, she nodded, setting the card on the kitchen counter beside her.

Odd how such a small victory had him feeling like he'd won the Super Bowl. "Reckon I oughta go get that Frisbee down so you and the little ones can get back to settling in."

"I suppose so," she said, her gaze taking in the room. "We have a bit of cleaning to do to make the bedrooms sleep-ready." She started from the room, limping slightly as she went.

"Your calf okay?" he asked as he followed.

"Starting to feel a little tender."

"Try not to baby it," he said. "I know it's uncomfortable to walk on, but you have to keep that calf muscle stretched out."

"I think you went into the wrong line of work, Mr. Cooper," she said, flashing a smile back at him over her shoulder. "You really should have been a doctor."

"I was a volunteer firefighter for a couple of years after I graduated from high school, during which time I received training in first aid, but my true calling is construction."

"I have to wonder," she said with a smile.

He let out a husky laugh. "Trust me. These hands are far better off hammering nails than tending to patients. I'm blue collar through and through." Reaching past her, he opened the screen door, holding it until she was safely out on the porch. Then he stepped out behind her.

"But you own your company," she replied. "Wouldn't that make you more white collar?"

"Not for a second," he answered honestly. "I work right alongside my crew doing any type of physical labor the job calls for. The work can be hard. It can be dirty. And, on occasion, dangerous."

"I—"

"Here you go," Lily hollered as she raced up onto the porch, ending any further discussion about his chosen occupation. Smiling, she held out the bottle of water she and her brother had gone to retrieve for him.

"Thanks."

"Mommy," Mason said, following right behind. His mouth was drawn down into a worried frown. "The cooler is leaking."

She sighed tiredly. "The plug must have come loose again."

"While you see to the cooler," Carter said, "I'll go grab a more reliable ladder from my truck and get that Frisbee down."

"You might as well leave it up there," Lily told him.

He glanced down at her. "You don't want me to get it down so you can play with it?"

"It'll just go up there again," she said, glancing toward her brother. "Mason's not a good thrower."

The boy's brows drew together at his sister's insult. "I'm a better thrower than you are!"

"Children," Audra admonished.

"It's true," her son said. "I wish I had someone to throw with that knows how to play Frisbee."

"Your sister tries her best," she said calmly.

"I don't like to throw," Lily said, her bottom lip pulling downward into a pout.

It was clear to see feelings were about to get hurt. "Not everyone does," he assured her. "You're probably really good at tea parties."

Her little face lit up. "I am!"

He offered her a smile and then looked to Mason. "My niece, Katydid, who's about your age I would guess, loves to play Frisbee. I'll have to introduce you to her since you're gonna be living here."

The boy's expression was priceless—wide-eyed and openmouthed, displaying a small gap where two of his bottom baby teeth had once been. "She's named after a bug?"

Carter chuckled. "Not really. Katydid is what I call her. Her real name is Katherine Marie, but everyone calls her Katie."

"Mommy, the van's raining!" Lily exclaimed in a high-pitched squeal.

They all turned to see water spilling out from behind the sliding passenger door the kids had left partially open.

Audra gasped. "Oh, no! Excuse me," she called back as she broke into a run for her van.

Carter watched her go. *Lord,* he thought to himself, *if anyone needs a little extra help, it's her.* Not that she'd accept it. Audra Marshall was determined to go it on her own. Stubborn female.

"I'm hungry," Lily whined, drawing Audra's gaze across what would be the master bedroom, to where her young daughter had settled herself onto the freshly scrubbed hardwood floor. Arms crossed. Bottom lip pushed out in a pout.

Her baby girl was exhausted. Understandably

so. The three of them had worked hard the past few hours, sweeping and scrubbing down the kids' rooms, along with the upstairs bathroom and part of the kitchen, all of which had been monumental tasks. The rest of the cleaning could wait until the next day, her own room included. At least the floor was clean, even if the walls weren't. She cast a fretful glance around the room, taking in its faded, peeling wallpaper and scuffed-up hardwood floor, and felt the overwhelming urge to cry. *Lord, please give me the strength to do what needs to be done here.*

At least they would have a roof over their heads, albeit a slightly sunken one, but a roof all the same. Her children would have clean rooms to sleep in, free of dust motes and cobwebs. And while she'd given the kitchen a fairly thorough scrubbing, Audra didn't have the strength left to make use of it and cook dinner for the three of them.

She looked toward the sleeping bag she'd unrolled, where the bed would be. It was only for one night. The moving truck with her oversize storage containers was scheduled to arrive the following day and then she'd be able to get their beds set up and make the place look more like a home.

"Mommy," her daughter pleaded woefully.

Audra managed a tired smile. "Why don't

we wash up, then take a ride into town to get something to eat?"

Her daughter's eyes lit up. "Can we get a big dog?"

The big dog her daughter was referring to was the hot-dog shop they had passed by in town when they'd arrived in Braxton. A place called Big Dog's. She had to admit it wasn't exactly the healthiest choice for their overly late dinner, but her daughter had worked hard. If Lily wanted a hot dog for dinner, she was going to have one.

"Go down and wake your brother. Tell him to come inside and wash his face and change his shirt before we go."

"Okay!" Lily sprang to her feet and raced from the room.

"You, too!" she called after her.

Moments later, the front screen door creaked open and then banged shut. Mason had volunteered to carry the trash bucket downstairs whenever it got full and out to the two battered aluminum garbage cans they'd found out back. He was exhausted as well and had curled up on the porch swing some forty minutes or so earlier, falling fast asleep.

Audra bent to grab on to the handle of the scrub bucket, carrying it and the mop she'd been using into the bathroom. Her arms ached.

Her back ached. And this was only the beginning. The thought of everything that needed to be done was emotionally overwhelming. Her children deserved so much better than this. If only she had known what they would be getting into. But she hadn't. Just as she hadn't known the man she'd pledged her love to years before would walk away from the faith they had shared, the love they had shared, the family they had shared.

Had shared, because Bradford had chosen to give up all legal rights to Mason and Lily. No, he had insisted, been determined to free himself from the... How had he put it? The *baggage* he'd saddled himself with? That was how Bradford Marshall regarded the family he had created. As baggage. He'd given them all up without an ounce of regret. And for what? Another woman. One who, like Bradford, didn't want to be tied down with the responsibilities of being a parent.

In the end, the decision had been up to Audra as to whether or not she would release him from his parental rights, which in their case was nothing more than the financial support Bradford was required to give to her children after the divorce. Payments he failed to make, leaving Audra to provide sole financial support for their children. So after many hours spent in prayer and some very tear-filled visits with their preacher, she came to the decision to allow Bradford to cut all ties with her children. Forcing him to stay a part of their lives would only make him more resentful toward Mason and Lily. They would have been forced to endure more of Bradford's constant criticism, his unprovoked anger and, worst of all, his icy indifference.

Audra swiped at her dirt-smudged cheek to brush away the telltale trail of moisture, not wanting her children to see her crying. Her heart ached. Not for the loss of her marriage. That had ended long before anything had been finalized legally. But for her children. They deserved a father who would cherish them. What they had gotten was a man who had considered them hindrances to the life he wanted to live.

"Lily said we're going for hot dogs."

She turned to find a sleepy-eyed Mason standing in the bathroom doorway. "As soon as we get cleaned up," she said, forcing herself to pull it together. She looked past her son. "Where's your sister?"

"Waiting in the van," he replied with a yawn.

Rolling her eyes, she started for the door. "Scrub your face while I go get Lily. And be sure to change into a clean shirt." She headed outside to get her daughter. She understood

Lily's need for a real meal. The snacks they'd eaten while taking breaks from their cleaning had helped to tide them over, but only temporarily. But Audra wasn't about to take either of her children into town looking like ragamuffins. She'd already made a very poor first impression on one of Braxton's residents.

The memory of Carter Cooper's "masked" face managed to bring a smile to her own. But only for a moment, before she remembered he was the kind of man she needed to steer clear of. Kind and charming, and from what she could see of his face, quite handsome, as well. All of the things Bradford had been, and look where that led her.

Pushing all thoughts of her ex *and* Carter Cooper from her mind, Audra made her way out to the van, where Lily sat buckled in the backseat, door open while she waited for them to join her.

"I'm ready to go," Lily whined.

"Honey, I know you're hungry," she said sympathetically. "We all are. But you need to go back inside and wash up before can we go."

Her daughter frowned. "Can't I wash up there?"

"Most restaurants prefer their diners to come in somewhat clean," she explained. "Not with bits of cobweb clinging to their clothes and dirt smudged on their faces."

Lily looked down at her shirt and gave a tiny sigh as she released the belt securing her in the seat. "Okay."

Smiling, Audra followed her back into the house.

Twenty minutes later, looking far more presentable, they pulled into one of the empty parking spaces in front of Big Dog's. Of which there were plenty. Considering it was nearly eight o'clock at night, the mostly empty street didn't surprise her.

Audra's gaze zeroed in on the restaurant-hours sign in the door and relief swept through her. Big Dog's was open until 10:00 p.m. Lily would have been so disappointed if they'd had to go somewhere else and she'd already disappointed her children enough. Not that they'd ever voiced any such thing, but it was how she felt inside.

Her children were out of the van and waiting at the entrance to the restaurant before Audra had even shut off the engine.

"Hurry up, Mommy!" Lily called out, dancing around in excitement.

Where had that burst of energy come from? Audra wondered. She certainly had none left in her. Smiling, she reached for her purse and then stepped from the van, locking it behind her.

Mason was standing in front of one of the large plate glass windows, peering in.

"Honey, it's not polite to stare in the window like that," she told him as she joined them on the sidewalk. "People are trying to eat."

"No one's in there," he told her as he moved toward the door.

"Still," she said, "we don't do that." Audra pulled open the door, holding it as her children scampered excitedly inside. A young waitress came over to greet them.

"Welcome to Big Dog's," she said with a warm smile. "Sit anywhere you like and I'll go grab some menus."

"Over here," Lily said, hurrying toward a booth by the window, two away from the door.

Mason took a seat on the opposite side of the table while Audra slid in next to her daughter.

The waitress, a young woman who looked to be in her early twenties with long strawberry-blond hair and a sprinkling of freckles across her nose and cheeks, returned carrying three glasses of ice water and menus, which she promptly handed out. Then she held up two smaller menus. "I brought along a couple of children's menus just in case. The hot dogs on the main menu are for those wanting really big hot dogs. The ones on the kids menu are regular size."

"Thank you," Audra said. "But something tells me we'll all be ordering from the regular menu tonight."

"'Cause we're starving," Lily informed her in dramatic fashion.

The younger woman laughed at her daughter's antics. "You are, are you?"

"We missed dinner tonight," Audra explained. "We just moved into the Harris place and had some cleaning to do. It took a little longer than we thought it would."

"The Harris place?" the waitress repeated, her expression matching the one Carter Cooper had on his face when he'd learned Audra had bought the place. "That old abandoned house out on Red Oak Road?"

"That would be the one," Audra said, reaching for one of the menus.

"You've got your work cut out for you there," she said. "If you're looking to hire someone on to help out there, I could give you the number for our local contractors."

"Would that happen to be Cooper Construction?"

"You've already hired them on," the girl replied, sounding almost relieved. "Smart move.

They're the best there is in these parts when it comes to renovations."

Audra knew she should have cleared things up as far as her hiring Carter's company was concerned, but she didn't want to explain that she couldn't afford to have her house renovated by professionals.

The front door opened at that moment, saving Audra from having to say anything more. She did a double take, thinking the man who had just stepped into the restaurant was none other than Carter Cooper. But on closer inspection, this man was even taller than the cowboy who had come to her rescue that afternoon, and slightly leaner. Carter Cooper was more broad-shouldered and had the extra bulk of muscle on his frame that had most likely come from all the physical labor involved in working construction.

"Hey, Lizzie," the man said in greeting to the waitress.

"Hey, Logan."

His gaze shifted to the booth where Audra and her children sat. Tipping his cowboy hat with a polite smile, he said, "Ma'am." A smile that was an exact replica of Carter Cooper's unarguably handsome, slightly crooked grin. Only instead of sporting a mask of black around his eyes, he had smudges of dirt all over his face and clothes.

"How's come I had to wash my face before we came here?" Lily said, her words echoing loudly in the empty room. "He didn't."

Audra wanted to sink down into the booth and hide. Make that two bad first impressions with someone from Braxton in just one day.

The man chuckled. "Your momma has the right of it," he told Lily. "I'm just stopping by on my way home from work to pick up my dinner order. Unfortunately, my job requires me to play in dirt so this is how I usually look at the end of the day."

"I want to do that when I grow up," Mason announced.

"Me, too!" Lily squealed.

The man seemed thoroughly entertained by their reaction. "It's hard work," he said, his attention focused solely on her children.

"We're hard workers," Lily stated. "Aren't we, Mommy?"

"Very," she agreed with a nod.

"Your brothers are gonna be helping her with her new place."

His brothers? That explained the resemblance.

He looked Audra's way. "That so? Where's that?"

"The old Harris place," Lizzie answered for her.

His dark brows lifted in undeniable surprise.

"I know," Audra said before he could voice his thoughts. "It's a big job, but with a little tender loving care the house will be a home in no time." She had to wonder who she was truly trying to convince. Him or herself.

"If you all will excuse me," Lizzie said, "I'm gonna go grab Logan's order." Then she scurried off into the kitchen.

He looked to Audra. "If you need any help with the landscaping out there, just give me a shout. I own a landscaping business and join forces with my brothers on a lot of their jobs."

"How many Cooper brothers are there?" she said.

"Only three," he said, his grin widening. "I'm the youngest. Although I'm not so sure Carter's laying claim to me right now."

"Are you the one who painted his face?" Mason asked.

"Saw that, did you?" he said.

Her children nodded.

"Actually, it was our older brother, Nathan, who did the *painting*. But it was sort of my idea," he admitted. "Mind you, it wasn't a very nice thing for us to do to him and it's not something either of you should ever do to anyone."

She was grateful that he didn't boast about the prank they'd pulled on their brother and had, instead, stressed to her highly impressionable young children that it was something that should never be repeated.

Lizzie returned, carrying a white paper bag, and walked over to the cash register. "You're all set," she told Logan.

"Pleasure to meet you," he said, tipping his hat once more before going over to pay for his order.

"How's come he wears that hat if it's too big?" Mason said in an attempted whisper. However, voices carried in the empty room and she was certain she heard Logan Cooper's muffled chuckle from across the room.

Keeping her own voice low, Audra explained, "It's not too big,"

"Then why does he keep pushing it up like that?" her son persisted.

"Because that's what cowboys do down here in Texas. It's how they show ladies respect."

"Then I need one, too," he said as he watched Logan leave with his order. "Just like his, so I can be a real cowboy."

Audra couldn't help but smile as she added a cowboy hat to her lists of things they needed for their new life in Braxton. Because more than anything she wanted to make certain her children were happy here and felt like they fit in.

Chapter Three

Logan glanced up from the hole he was digging and smiled. "What brings you out here?"

"The need to work," Carter answered honestly as he crossed the newly laid sod in front of Braxton's only bank, where his brother had been hired to do a complete external face-lift to the property. He'd spent most of the night tossing and turning, his thoughts filled with Audra Cooper and her two young children and that eyesore of a house they were going to be living in. Leaving them to handle things alone the afternoon before had really eaten at him. But what choice did he have? Audra had made it clear she didn't need his help. No, she definitely needed his help. It was that she didn't *want* his help. Even when it was freely offered.

"I would think you'd be enjoying your time off between jobs. Maybe doing a multiday hike up into the hills," his brother said as he went back to digging a hole for the ornamental tree he had sitting next to the spot.

Carter frowned. If only he could be enjoying his day off. And while hiking was a favorite pastime for him whenever he had the time, he knew if he'd gone up into the hills, relaxation was the last thing he'd find there. He would have spent all his time worrying over Braxton's newest residents. "Do you need any help here or not?" he asked in a rare show of impatience.

Logan simply laughed. "If you're that fired up to work, you could lend me a hand with the mulching."

"Fine," Carter grumbled.

"There's a wheelbarrow full of mulch around back," his brother told him. "You can start filling in around the trees and plants I've already put in."

With a nod, Carter set off around the building, his mouth in a grim line. While he'd come there hoping to distract himself from thoughts of Audra Marshall and her kids the exact opposite was happening. Looking at the newly laid lawn made him think about the jungle of grass and weeds surrounding the old Harris place. Did she have a mower? And if she did, would it be powerful enough to get through the deep grass? And what about that overgrown hedgerow? Did she have the tools needed to bring that out-of-control shrubbery into some semblance of order?

Spying the wheelbarrow, which had been heaped high with a deep red mulch, he walked over to it and proceeded to wheel it back around to the front side of the bank, where his brother was hard at work.

After a good twenty minutes or so of tossing shovelfuls of mulch onto the designated garden area, Logan said, "Is your offer to help me out here today your way of getting back at me for the goggle prank?"

Carter stopped what he was doing to cast a questioning glance his brother's way. "Why would you think that?" Truth was, getting back at his brother was the furthest thing from his mind at that moment. His thoughts were far too preoccupied by one very stubborn female.

"Considering how much of that mulch is ending up on the sod I just laid the day before, I'd say it's a pretty good guess."

His gaze dropped to the ground at his feet, where, sure enough, a growing pile of red mulch lay atop the bright green grass—a good foot away from the edge of the landscaped area he'd been helping Logan with.

With a groan, Carter set the shovel aside and knelt to clean up the mess he'd made, scooping the misplaced mulch up in his bare hands as not to damage the grass.

"You wanna tell me what's gnawing at you?" his brother asked as he settled onto his knees on the ground beside him.

"More like who," Carter mumbled with a frown as he tossed a handful of mulch into the flower bed, where it belonged.

"Who?" Logan repeated. "Look, if you're still upset with Nathan about what happened, keep in mind that he was only partially responsible for the shoe polish on your goggles."

"I'm not referring to Nathan," he said. "I'm referring to a stubborn female who's jumped off into the deep end and is now struggling to tread water."

"Afraid you've lost me there, big brother."

Carter scooped more of the misplaced mulch into a pile. "There's this woman who needs my help but is determined not to take it."

"Anyone I know?"

He shook his head. "No. She just moved to town."

"She wouldn't happen to be a tiny thing with golden-brown hair, two very inquisitive children and the new owner of the old Harris place?"

Carter's head snapped up, his gaze locking with his brother's. "How do you know Audra?"

"We met in passing last night at Big Dog's," Logan said, getting to his feet as the last of the mulch that could gather was removed from the grass. "Lizzie said you and Nathan were gonna be doing work out there."

"Not sure where Lizzie got that idea," he said with a frown as he stood. "Audra's determined to do most of the work on that place herself."

"By herself? You mean her and her husband?"

He shook his head. "Nope. I mean only her. She's divorced."

"I take it she has experience in home renovations then."

"Not a lick."

"So you're just gonna take no for an answer?" his brother challenged.

"I can't force her to allow me to help her."

His brother stepped back into the garden, retrieving his discarded shovel. "Reckon you could always blame Momma."

"Excuse me?"

His brother looked his way with a grin. "You and I both know Momma wouldn't be too pleased with us if we were to turn our backs on someone in need. And it sounds to me like Audra is clearly in need."

Carter's mood lightened instantly. "Good point. Last thing I'd wanna do is let Momma down.

His brother's crooked grin lifted even more. "Exactly."

"Uncle Carter!" Katie squealed as she raced out of the house to greet him.

Carter swept her up in his arms and spun her around like he'd done since she was a toddler. "Katydid," he chuckled. It warmed his heart every time he saw her. It also reminded him of how fortunate he and his brothers were to still have her there with them. A true blessing in their lives.

"I'm getting dizzy," she said with a giggle.

"No," he said, lowering her carefully to her feet, "what you're getting is big. Sprouting up like a weed."

She looked up at him. "I'm not a weed. Daddy says I'm a sunflower 'cause I'm getting so tall and I like tipping my face up to the sun."

He reached down to playfully pinch her tiny cheek. "That explains where all these sun kisses came from."

"Those aren't from the sun," she told him. "They're from my mommy."

A lump wedged in his throat at the mention

of Isabel. His sister-in-law had been a wonderful, loving mother. She should be there raising her daughter alongside Nathan. His only comfort was in knowing that his sister-in-law was safe in the Lord's loving arms. No doubt keeping watch over his beautiful little niece.

"Looks like you forgot something in the house," he said, his gaze zeroing in on her mouth.

"I did?" she replied.

He nodded. "Your teeth."

Her tongue moved to the empty space where two of her bottom teeth used to be. "Oh, those," she said. "I lost them."

"You need help looking for them?" he teased.

"Not that kind of lost." She giggled. "Daddy says I'm gonna start losing my teeth 'cause my big-girl teeth are getting ready to come in."

"Where is your daddy?" he asked with a forced smile.

"Nana Mildred needed some wood, so Daddy drove around back to load some in his truck."

Mildred Timmons had been his parents' neighbor for nearly forty years. Her husband had been the only other casualty from the tornado that struck Braxton, leaving behind a wide path of destruction that the town was still trying to recover from. Millie looked after Katie for his brother when Nathan was at work and had become a much-loved surrogate grand-mother to his niece. It helped to ease Millie's loneliness and gave Katie some much-needed female presence in her life. Probably the only she would ever have seeing as how Nathan was dead set against ever marrying again.

"Reckon I'll take a walk around back, then," he told her. "You want a piggyback ride?"

She shook her head, her dark curls bouncing about on her slender shoulders. "Daddy said I'm supposed to wait at the house until he's done chopping wood."

"Then you best do what your daddy says," he said. Nathan was overprotective of his little girl and understandably so. Losing Isabel had crushed his brother both spiritually and emo-tionally. If anything were to happen to Katie... Carter shook the thought away. "I'll be back in to see you before I go."

"Okay, Uncle Carter," she said with a smile. "See you in a bit."

He waited until she'd gone back into the house before setting off in search of his brother. Nathan's property consisted of just under two acres of mowed backyard and side yard with a few scattered oaks that butted up against a large expanse of woods, which his brother also owned. In the backyard was a rather impres-sive wooden swing set/jungle gym his brother had built for Katie, a miniature castle playhouse and a large pole barn.

The sound of wood being stacked onto wood drew Carter's gaze toward the pole barn. He spotted his brother's truck, backed up to the towering pile of firewood Nathan had recently replenished with his and Logan's help. His brother was standing in the bed of the truck, stacking the split logs he'd loaded onto it.

Carter started across the yard in lengthened strides.

Nathan glanced up, a slow smile moving across his tanned face. "Almost didn't recognize you without your mask."

"You're hilarious," Carter muttered as he stepped up alongside the truck bed. "Took me nearly an hour to get the stuff off my face when I got home and only with the help of some solvent-based cleaner they recommended at the hardware store. Mind you, that was only *after* they had a good laugh at my expense, saying they were sure I was a masked robber when I first stepped into the store."

His brother threw back his head, his husky laughter cutting into the silence of the nature surrounding them. "Thanks for sharing that little tidbit. That just made my day."

"Logan's rubbing off on you," Carter muttered. "And I don't mean in a good way." Despite the semiscowl he'd plastered on his face, it was good to hear his brother's laughter. It had been a rare thing since losing Isabel, with the exception of when his brother was around Katie. His daughter always seemed to bring a smile to Nathan's face.

"So what brings you out here this evening?" his brother asked. "Come to get more revenge? Because I'll tell you, you had me sweating it when you had me thinking you'd put my keys in that bucket of primer."

"Good. You deserved to sweat a little."

"Hey, I wasn't the lone man in that prank."

"Don't you worry. Logan's gonna get his," Carter said. "I'm just biding my time."

Nathan walked down to the end of the truck bed and settled himself down onto the open tailgate, dangling his long legs over the edge. "Meaning you haven't come up with something as good as the prank he had me pull on you?"

Carter grinned. "Exactly. Besides, I'd like to pay him back when he's least expecting it. As for why I'm here, I need a door. Do you still have the ones we salvaged from the Parker renovation we did last fall?"

His brother nodded. "In the pole barn. Why?"

"There's a lady in sore need of a halfway decent door. Figured I'd give her one of those since we don't really have any plans for them."

Nathan quirked a dark brow. "You're doing a side job?"

He understood his brother's curiosity. They were partners and always worked as a team. Even on the small jobs. "I wouldn't exactly call it a job." How did he explain it? That he met a woman, a pretty one at that, rescued her actually, and then offered his services, which she promptly turned down. Now he couldn't stop thinking about her, and wanted to do something to help her out?

"Are you gonna make me drag it out of you?" his brother muttered impatiently.

"She's new to Braxton," he explained. "Just arrived yesterday, as a matter of fact."

"So you're giving her a used door as a housewarming gift?"

"I'm giving her the door because she can't afford a new one," Carter said with a frown. "Not with everything she has to do to the old Harris place."

His brother threw up a hand. "Hold up. Did you just say the old Harris place?"

He nodded. "Bought it sight unseen from an online auction."

The face Nathan made said it all. "I haven't been by that place for a nearly a year, but last time I was the old house was practically begging someone to bring in a wrecking ball and put it out of its misery and put something new up in its place."

"That's the thing," Carter said with a frown. "Audra has no intention of tearing the place down. She intends to live there."

His brother's dark brow lifted even farther. "Audra?"

"With her children," he added, so his brother wouldn't think this had anything to do with her being a prettier-than-most female.

"Grown-up children?" his brother persisted.

He shook his head. "I'd say they're closer to Katie in age. And before you ask, she's divorced. Her ex sounds like a real loser."

"Are you passing judgment on someone you've never met? Not like you, little brother."

"He chose to give up all rights to his children," he said. "And they're pretty hurt by it."

Nathan looked aghast. "Those poor kids. So where are they staying while the house is being renovated?"

"I believe they're gonna be staying in the house."

His brother's blue eyes widened. "That's gonna make it a challenge for anyone she does bring in to help out with the bigger jobs."

Carter's frown deepened. "That's not gonna be an issue. She's got it in her pretty little head to do most of the repairs herself."

"Pretty, huh?"

Carter groaned. "Did you hear what I just said? She's gonna try and fix that old house up all by herself."

"Heard that," his brother replied. "But it's the *pretty* part I'm latching on to. That's gotta be the first female in a long while you've taken notice of."

"Hard not to notice her when I had to rescue her from a roof."

"You what?"

With a sigh, he went on to explain what he'd stumbled upon the previous afternoon. "She's in over her head."

"And you're gonna come to her rescue again?" his brother said, studying him closely.

"I'd do the same if it were an old woman," Carter said, feeling the need to defend himself. But he doubted an older woman would have plagued his thoughts the way Audra Marshall and her children had since he'd left their place. "So about that door…"

Nathan motioned toward the pole barn. "Have at it. Just watch you're not the one who ends up in over your head. And I'm not referring to the renovations to her house."

"No worry there," Carter called back over his shoulder as he started for the entry door to the pole barn. "I like my life just the way it is." No family of his own to worry about losing far too soon, like Nathan had. He'd seen what his brother went through, was still going through, and he never wanted to stand in his shoes. So while he dated on occasion, he made sure the women he went out with knew he wasn't looking for a long-term relationship. Just someone to grab dinner with or see a movie.

Nothing more.

"What in the world?" For the second time in two days, Carter found himself barreling up Audra Marshall's driveway in his truck.

Lodged within the frame of the open front door was what looked to be a box spring. Behind it, attempting to push it into the house, were Audra and her young son. Lily stood off to the side, happily cheering them on.

Carter threw the truck into Park and leaped out.

"It's the Lone Ranger!" Lily exclaimed, jumping up and down in excitement.

Audra paused to look back over her shoulder. "Mr. Cooper," she greeted between the labored pants of her determined efforts.

"Looks like I got here just in time," he said as he stepped up onto the porch.

"What are you doing here?" she demanded as she reached up to push a strand of hair that had come loose from her ponytail away from her face. She looked oddly adorable in her rumpled, oversize #1 MOM T-shirt that practically swallowed up her petite form, knee-length leggings and hot-pink tennis shoes. Not that he ought to be noticing those things.

"I came to do my Christian duty," he said, reaching past her to grab hold of the box spring.

"We don't—"

"Need my help?" he said, arching a challenging brow.

She bit at her bottom lip.

"Now that we got that settled, let's get this thing through the doorway."

"It won't fit," Lily told him.

"Sure it will, little darlin', but not at this angle." He looked to Audra. "I'll need to shift it slightly and then we should be able to ease it through." His gaze focused on Mason. "I'll need your help with this, big guy. Think you could crawl in through that gap at the floor and tell us how much farther we need to push the box spring to get it all the way inside?"

"I can do that!" he replied.

"I'm not so sure that's a good idea," Audra said with a worried frown.

"Trust me," Carter told her. "This box spring isn't going anywhere the way it's sitting right now."

She eyed the gap between the door frame and the bottom portion of the box spring and then looked to her son. "Watch you don't bump your head going through there."

"I will," her little boy replied. A second later, he was scooting through the narrow hole.

Carter kept a firm hold on the box spring until Mason had cleared the doorway. Then he adjusted the box spring with an ease neither Audra nor her children could have managed. "It's best he stay out of the way while I take this through," he whispered for her ears only.

She looked up at him, understanding dawning. "I appreciate your taking my son's well-being into consideration," she whispered back, her voice catching slightly.

"How are we looking on your side, Mason?" he called out to her son.

"All clear!"

"Okay, coming through." With a powerful nudge of his shoulder, he worked the box spring in through the open door. Then he managed, with some maneuvering and a little help from Audra, to get it upstairs to her room. He did the same with the mattress. Then he turned to the kids. "Time to bring your beds up."

"They're already up here," Lily said.

He looked to Audra, who nodded. "You got them upstairs by yourself?"

She smiled. "They're only twin-size and Mason helped."

"I did, too, Mommy," Lily whined.

"Yes, she did, too," her mother quickly amended. "Lily carried up their pillows."

"I see," Carter said with a nod. "My next question is, why didn't the movers carry your things inside for you?"

"I didn't hire movers," she admitted. "I just hired a company to store our things and then deliver them to the house the day after we got here. We're supposed to unload everything and they'll send someone to pick up their storage pods in two days."

Reaching up, he dragged a sleeve across his damp brow. "Two days?"

She nodded.

"Then you're gonna need help moving your things in before the rain gets here."

"Rain?" she gasped.

"It's expected to hit tomorrow afternoon," he told her. "And according to the local weather station it's gonna be hanging around a spell."

"I'll just have to work faster getting things inside," she said determinedly, her response not surprising him one bit.

"Darlin', there's a time for holding on firm to our pride and there's a time for swallowing it," he told her as he pulled his cell phone from the front pocket of his jeans and punched in Nathan's number.

"What are you doing?" she asked, her gaze dropping to the phone in his hand.

His mouth pulled up into a grin as he replied, "Calling for backup."

Chapter Four

Calling for backup? What did he think he was doing? "Carter," she said, trying to get his attention.

He motioned for her to give him a second and then said into the phone as he walked away from the porch, "Remember that little prank you and Logan pulled on me the other day…"

"Mommy," Lily said, tugging at the bottom of Audra's T-shirt, "are we done?"

If only. There was so much to do before the rain came in. The cardboard boxes she'd packed things into had to be taken inside. If they sat out in the yard, they'd be nothing but mush, because the storage containers would be leaving. "You can take a little break if you'd like," she said, her gaze still fixed on Carter Cooper's broad shoulders as he stood in her yard, talking away on his cell phone.

"Can we go explore?" Mason asked.

Audra looked down at her son, nodding. "Don't go far and stay away from the pond."

"Okay," her children replied before leaping off the porch.

She watched them go with a wistful smile. The Lord had blessed her with two wonderful children. Both loving and happy despite the past hurts they'd suffered. They deserved time to play and have fun like other children. "Keep an eye on your sister!" she called after her son.

"I will!" Mason hollered back before he and Lily disappeared around the side of the house.

Her attention shifted back to Carter Cooper to find him shoving his cell phone into the front pocket of his jeans. With a smile that made her wonder what he was up to, he walked back to where she stood waiting.

"Help is on the way."

"Mr. Cooper," she said in frustration.

"Carter," he said. "Mr. Cooper was my daddy."

"Fine. Carter," she began again with a worried frown. "I don't want to impose on you or anyone else."

"It's called helping a neighbor," he replied. "We tend to do a lot of that in these parts. Besides, my brothers owe me for the black eyes I was forced to walk around with yesterday. As far as I'm concerned, they're getting off easy."

It was clear he was determined to do this. How could she refuse? He'd come to her rescue, not once but twice. If Carter wanted to teach his brothers a lesson by having them help move her things into the house, then she owed it to him to let them do so. "Only if they're willing to help," she conceded.

"Oh, they're willing," he replied before turning to make his way over to one of the open storage containers. "Reckon we best get started."

We. How long had it been since another adult included her in something? As if they were a team. Had Bradford ever used the term *we*? No. He was more likely to say "I" or "me." Realizing that she was dwelling on a past she'd just as soon forget, Audra pushed away all thoughts of her ex and joined Carter inside one of the storage containers.

He glanced her way with a grin. "Impressive organization."

He was referring to the notes she'd made on the outside of each box, which included room placement and a list of the items inside. Warmth filled her cheeks. "Old habits die hard."

He chuckled. "You say that like it's a bad thing to be organized."

"It can be," she admitted as she reached for one of the smaller boxes that contained pantry items. Her ex-husband had complained that she wasn't more go-with-the-flow. That everything she did was too scheduled and regimented. But she had to be. How else would she have kept up with the dance classes Bradford had insisted Lily be enrolled in. Or the T-ball and youth soccer teams that Mason had joined.

"I'm not so sure my older brother would agree with that statement," he said with a chuckle. "He's always getting on me about my need to be more organized. Must be a skill people with children acquire, because my younger brother, Logan, is almost as bad as me when it comes to that sort of thing."

She nodded with a smile. "It must be."

"What would you like me to bring in first?"

"The box with the sheets and blankets in it," she said, pointing to a cardboard box near the bottom of one of the stacks.

"Sheets and blankets it is." He removed two boxes that were on top of the bedding box and then lifted it, along with the box below it, also marked bedroom, into his muscular arms.

Audra followed him inside. "You can place those on the floor in the first bedroom. I'll run this box into the kitchen."

He did so without hesitation, moving up the steps as if the boxes he carried weighed nothing at all. Then again, the man was a veritable giant.

She sat the box she'd carried inside onto the floor by the pantry door. She would have to wait to unpack their dry goods until she'd had a chance to paint inside the shelf-lined closet. Hopefully, in the next day or so.

By the time she returned to the entryway, Carter was already outside and moving toward the open storage container. She hurried to catch up to him. "Carter…"

He slowed his step, glancing over at her from beneath the brim of his hat. "Darlin'?"

Darlin'. Why did he have to call her that? It added a touch of intimacy to their relationship that didn't belong. They were strangers. He knew nothing about her. Well, beyond the fact that she was divorced and a poor judge of men. And while she was at it, she might as well toss poor judge of houses into the mix.

"Why are you doing this?" she demanded uneasily. Guilt nagged at her for taking up his valuable time even though she hadn't asked it of him. Did he think his lending a hand would convince her to hire him on?

He smiled. An adorably crooked grin that made her stomach flutter ever so slightly. "Because sometimes folks, myself included, need a little help and are too proud to ask for it."

She looked past him, focusing on the moving bins. It wasn't pride that kept her from asking.

It was experience. Asking her ex for something had rarely gotten her anywhere. She'd eventually learned that if she wanted something done, she needed to do it herself. Even if in doing so she sometimes found herself completely out of her realm of comfort and, as of more recently, her ability.

"I…" Her denial that she needed his help died on her lips as she glanced toward the boxes and large pieces of furniture filling the open containers. There was no getting around it, she thought with a frown. She needed help.

"Audra," he said with a sigh, the sound of her name on his lips drawing her gaze upward. "Let me do this for you. Not for money. Not for any of the reasons I have a feeling you're tossing around in your head. But because…well, I'm the Lone Ranger," he said. "And the Lone Ranger would never leave a female in need." Then, as if his crazy explanation made all the difference, he strode off to the moving container.

Unable to help herself, she smiled, calling out, "So, if you're the Lone Ranger, where's your sidekick?" The question had no sooner left her lips when two pickup trucks turned up her drive.

Carter's head popped out around the open

door and a grin spread across his face. "Looks like my sidekicks have arrived."

She stood watching as the trucks came to a stop in a single line behind Carter's. A second later, two very large men in cowboy hats stepped out of them. The taller and leaner of the two she recognized from Big Dog's. Logan Cooper. The other man, who had the same broad shoulders as Carter, had to be their older brother, Nathan. He walked around to the other side of his truck and swung open the passenger door. Tiny legs appeared beneath the door as the truck's other occupant climbed down. A second later, a little girl with a head full of long, dark curls appeared.

"Uncle Carter!" she called out excitedly the moment she spotted him standing at the entrance of the oversize moving container.

"Katydid!" He stepped down and started across the yard to greet her.

The little girl raced toward him with a pronounced limp, leaving the two men behind. She launched herself into Carter's outstretched arms. The love she had for her uncle was clearly returned, judging by the tenderness that came over his face as he held her.

Audra crossed the yard to stand next to them. "Hello," she said to Katie as Carter set her back on her feet.

"Hello," the little girl replied, with a smile that very much resembled Audra's son's with her two missing bottom teeth.

"Katie, I'd like you to meet Ms. Marshall. She just moved here to Braxton."

"Is my daddy gonna fix your house?" she asked as she stood staring up at the old farmhouse.

It was pretty bad when a child of maybe five or six years old could tell a house was in desperate need of repair. "I'm hoping to fix it up myself."

Curious dark eyes lifted to study Audra. "Do you have a hammer? 'Cause I have one you can borrow. It's pink."

Audra laughed softly. "That's very kind of you, Katie. I'll be sure to keep that in mind."

"Heard there was a need for some *real* muscle here," Carter's younger brother, Logan, said with a grin as he and Nathan joined them in the yard.

Carter let out a husky chuckle. "You heard right. And since the ladies' knitting club was already committed elsewhere, I called you two. Next best thing, I reckon."

Audra couldn't help but smile as she listened to their playful banter. An only child, she'd missed out on this sort of playful camaraderie with a sibling.

Nathan Cooper looked her way with a polite nod. "Ma'am."

"Ms. Marshall," Logan greeted with a tip of his hat.

"Reckon some introductions are needed. Audra, this is my brother Nathan."

Her smile widened. "It's nice to meet you."

He nodded. "Likewise."

"And I believe you've already met our little brother, Logan," Carter continued, motioning toward the youngest Cooper.

"Who tops you by a good two inches," Logan quickly pointed out.

"That he does," Nathan agreed with a nod.

"At 6'4" there are very few men he doesn't look down to," Carter said with a glance Logan's direction.

He was definitely tall. They were all tall, for that matter. So much so, Audra had to crane her neck to look up at them. Smiling at Logan, she said, "Nice to see you again."

"Same here. Reckon we'll be seeing a whole lot more of each other seeing as how you're gonna be living in Braxton."

"Daddy," Katie said, tugging at Nathan's hand. "Where are the kids Uncle Carter said I could play with?"

"They're around back," Carter replied. Then his gaze lifted to Audra. "I hope you don't mind. I figured we'd have enough manpower for the move that the kids would be able to play and get to know each other."

Katie turned pleading eyes in Audra's direction. "Can I play with them? Please…"

How could she refuse that sweet little face? Her children would welcome the opportunity to make a new friend. "Mason and Lily will love having a new playmate. Why don't I walk you around back and introduce you to them?"

Katie looked to her father. "Can I, Daddy?"

"Go on, cupcake," Nathan said with a warm smile, giving his daughter's curls a playful tousle. "Have fun."

"I will!" she said excitedly before turning to slip her hand into Audra's.

"I won't be long," Audra told them as she led Katie away in search of Mason and Lily.

"In the meantime," Carter called out to her, "my *sidekicks* and I will start unloading the furniture."

"Sidekicks?" she heard his brothers repeat in unison.

Audra muffled a giggle. Carter Cooper was a very silly man. A quality she found surprisingly endearing. "Mason and Lily are going to be so excited to meet you," she told Katie, forcing her thoughts away from her very distracting uncle. "Your uncle Carter tells me you're really good at throwing a Frisbee."

"I am," she said with pride.

As they rounded the back of the house, they came upon Audra's children, who were kicking a ball back and forth across the yard, which was clearly in need of a thorough mowing. Another thing to add to the rapidly growing "things to buy" list—an easily workable lawn mower.

"Kids, come meet Katie Cooper."

They stopped what they were doing to look her way. Then, a second later, ball abandoned, her children raced toward them.

Mason reached them first, his gaze fixed on their unexpected guest. "Are you Katydid?"

"Sure am," she replied with a nod.

"Hello," Lily said, moving past her brother. "Want to play kick the ball with us?"

Seeing her daughter's face fill with excitement at having a new friend made Audra's heart warm. Moving to Texas had meant saying goodbye to their friends in Chicago. Katie Cooper could help ease their transition to their new life there in Braxton.

"I can't."

Audra's gaze shifted to Katie, whose brilliant smile had suddenly withered. "Sure you can," she assured her.

"We could teach you how to play," Mason volunteered enthusiastically.

The little girl's smile sagged even further. "My daddy said I can't kick things or jump a lot because my leg is still healing."

Now it was Audra's turn to frown. She had seen Katie limping. She should have considered that playing ball might not be a good idea. She knelt down in front of Katie and forced a smile, pushing aside the guilt she felt at her unintentional thoughtlessness. "Then by all means you shouldn't be playing kickball right now. Maybe someday soon."

"Maybe so." She sighed.

"What happened to your leg, sweetie?"

"The house crushed it."

Her children's eyes widened at Katie's unexpected response.

Audra looked at her in confusion. "The house?"

"Like when the house landed on the witch in Oz?" Mason gasped.

Katie appeared to mull her son's question over, before replying, "Reckon so. Only it wasn't Dorothy's house that landed on me and my mommy. It was my Grammy and Pappy's house."

Before Audra could respond, Lily shrieked, drawing all their gazes her way. Her daughter was pointing to the deep grass a couple of feet behind Audra and Katie.

"Stay very still," she told Katie, her heart pounding. Thankfully her two children were out of striking range. "Mason, move your sister away," she said stiffly, her gaze pinned on the coiled-up snake. *Dear Lord, help me keep this child safe.*

The snake, clearly irritated by their presence, raised its head as if preparing to attack. Her first and only thought at that point was to get Katie out of striking distance. Shooting to her feet, she swept Katie up, racing away from the deadly snake with a speed that surprised even herself.

"Katie!" a deep, very worried male voice called out.

"Daddy!" she said as she clung to Audra's neck.

"What happened?" she heard Carter ask, sounding nearly as panicked as his brother as all three Cooper brothers raced toward them.

Nathan reached out, taking his daughter from Audra.

She bent, gasping for breath as anxiety constricted her lungs. "R-rattler," she spluttered, pointing toward the spot where she and Katie had been standing only moments before.

"Was she bit?" Nathan asked, his hands frantically searching his daughter's tiny limbs.

"No," she told him.

"Were you?" Carter said with a deepening frown as his gaze moved over her.

"Neither of us was bit," she assured him.

"Ms. Marshall saved me," Katie announced.

Carter stepped past them, moving in long strides toward the angry snake. Logan followed.

"Rat snake," she heard Logan say.

"Thought it might be," Carter confirmed.

Nathan let out a sigh of relief.

Relief she didn't feel in the least. Heart still pounding, she called out, "Don't you dare get bit by that snake, Carter Cooper!"

Logan looked her way, dark brow lifted.

"You, either," she added, her cheeks warming with embarrassment. She hadn't meant to leave him out when she'd voiced her concern. Carter's name just came out. "I don't want either of you getting hurt. Besides, I don't even know if my home owners insurance covers venomous snakebites."

"Darlin'," Carter said with a grin, "rat snakes aren't poisonous. And they're usually pretty timid. They only act like this when they're feeling threatened."

"You gave it a scare," Logan said with a nod.

She snorted. "I gave *it* a scare?" Her gaze shifted to the snake, which was still curled up and shaking its tail in a menacing manner.

Nathan lowered Katie to the ground. "Logan, why don't you move that snake on out of here while we take the children around front?"

Logan nodded and then walked over to a nearby tree, picking up a stick from the ground.

"Come on, kids," Nathan said, motioning for them to follow as he started back around to the front of the house, his daughter's hand tucked securely in his much larger one.

Mason and Lily scurried after them, not the least bit affected by their close encounter with the snake.

"Thank You, Lord," Audra muttered quietly.

Carter's gaze remained fixed on Audra. She had risked her own life, or would have if the snake had been poisonous, to save his niece. The very niece he'd promised Isabel to keep safe. He closed the distance between them.

"You okay?" he asked, noting the slight trembling in her hands as she stood watching the children go.

She turned, her teary gaze lifting to his face. "Well," she said, managing a smile, "I can breathe again. That's a start."

He offered a sympathetic smile. "Breathing is good."

The laughter that left her lips surprised him. Soft. As if releasing the tension that had filled her only moments before. "You and your brothers must think I'm silly for panicking the way I did. But snakes are far from commonplace where we used to live."

"You'll definitely find more out here in the country. Especially when the grass is high. Not having any real knowledge of snakes, you were right to be skittish of it."

Biting at her bottom lip, she glanced around the unmowed yard. "Looks like a push mower is at the top of my need-to-buy list."

"Push-mowing a yard this size could take hours. I'd suggest purchasing a riding mower instead."

"I'll take that into consideration," she said almost worriedly.

"I take it you've never operated a riding mower before."

She shook her head. "I've never operated a mower of any kind. My ex-husband had a lawn-care service take care of all of that."

Carter fought the urge to frown. Did the man see to anything that was his?

"But I can learn," she added with a stubborn lift of her chin.

"I have no doubt," he acknowledged with a chuckle. The woman's determination could surely make up for any lack of skill. But the tasks needing seeing to were multiplying. "You might consider saving yourself the expense of buying a mower of any sort for the next couple of months and pay to have the lawn taken care of. You're gonna have enough work on your plate as it is."

"Maybe so, but lawn care isn't cheap," she countered.

"I'm pretty sure I can get you a deal." His gaze moved across the yard to where his brother was returning from disposing of the snake. "I happen to know the owner of the town's local landscaping service."

She followed his gaze. "Logan?"

Carter nodded and then looked down at Audra with a grin. "Did I mention that he still owes me for that black mask I was wearing yesterday?"

She laughed softly, her gaze now shifting to the subject of their conversation. "I believe you already used that to get him to help move my belongings into the house."

"Why do I feel like my ears should be burning?" his brother asked as he drew near.

"Because they should be," she assured him with a smile as Logan joined them.

His brother cast a questioning glance his way.

"I was suggesting she make use of your lawn-care services for the next few months to keep her time freed up for all the renovations she's planning to tackle on her own," Carter explained. "At the friends-and-family rate, of course."

"Carter," she chided, a faint blush filling her cheeks. Looking up at Logan, she said, "I never asked for a discount. And I certainly wouldn't want to impose on your time."

Logan exchanged a glance with Carter and then said, "You wouldn't have to ask. After the risk you took to keep our Katie out of harm's way, I'd insist on giving you my best rate."

"But she wasn't in any real danger."

"You didn't know that," Carter reminded her once more.

"As for your imposing on my time," his brother continued, "it's what I do for a living. Your yard won't take me any time at all with the commercial-grade mowers I have at the ready."

Face tilted upward, she let her gaze travel from Logan to him and then back to his brother. "All right," she said with a sigh. "But only at a fair price to you. I won't have you cutting your rate so much you're losing money. And only for a month or so. By then, I should have most of the more extensive work that needs to be done on the house completed and will be free to see to my own yard. Speaking of which, I've got work to do."

A month or so? Not only was the woman taking on more than she could chew, but she also had no concept whatsoever of the time her home renovations were going to require of her. Before Carter could set her straight, she was gone.

Logan sidled up beside him. "She's right pretty. And she's got herself some real backbone. A man's gotta admire that in a female."

Carter turned to his younger brother with a frown. "You can just get your mind off her backbone."

"The woman's brave enough to transplant herself and her two children to a place completely foreign to them," his brother said. "She's determined to tackle this ramshackle place on her own. And she faced down a mighty big rat snake without dropping into a dead faint. I like her."

So did he, Carter thought with a deepening frown. "She's also trying to pull her life back together after what sounds like a not-so-pleasant marriage, followed by a not-so-pleasant divorce. So liking her doesn't come into play here. Got it?"

Logan arched a brow. "Does that go for you, as well?"

It especially went for him. He wanted to do his Christian duty and help Audra out, but he wasn't about to allow himself to like her. Not in that way. He wasn't looking for any sort of emotional entanglement. He started toward the front of the house, his brother walking beside him. "I'm only here to give her a much-needed hand. Nothing more."

"You trying to convince me of that or yourself?"

Carter did what he always did when Logan attempted to push his buttons. He ignored him. They rounded the house and his gaze immediately sought out Audra, much to his own frustration. He didn't want to like her. Not even a little. But Lord help him, he did.

Audra was standing inside one of the open moving container, dispersing small boxes to the children, who were doing their part to help. Then, smiling, she followed them into the house.

"A little help in here would be nice," Nathan called out from inside another of the moving containers, where he stood holding an armful of colorful pillows.

"You can leave the heavy stuff to us," Logan told him with a grin. Looking to Carter, he said,

"How about you take the two yellow throw pillows and I'll take the two blue ones?"

"I'm not talking about these," Nathan grumbled with a frown. "I was referring to the sofa. I didn't want them falling onto the ground when we carry the sofa into the house."

"Smart thinking," Logan said as he stepped forward to take the brightly colored pillows from Nathan. "I'll make sure these make it into the house safely. You two can get the sofa. I'll even get the door for you."

Carter exchanged eye rolls with Nathan before they bent to lift the plush beige sofa and followed their younger brother into the house.

Audra met them in the entryway. "Can I help?"

"Logan might need a hand with those pillows," Carter said. "We'd hate for him to pull a muscle before he attempts the really heavy stuff."

Logan shot him a halfhearted scowl.

She smothered a giggle.

"We're good," Carter assured her.

"Where would you like this?" Nathan asked as he adjusted his grip on his end of the sofa.

"In here," she said, motioning them into the recently scrubbed-down living room. "Against the far wall would be great. If you don't need my help, I'll head back out to get another armload of boxes. The kids went upstairs to play Go Fish in Lily's room."

"We're good," Carter assured her, watching as she made her way out onto the porch.

"Any chance you could crane that neck of yours back around this way so we could get this here sofa set down where it's supposed to go?" Nathan grumbled with a hint of impatience.

"He can't help himself," Logan said with a chuckle. "He's smitten."

Carter snapped his head around, his dark brows drawn together. "I am *not* smitten."

His brothers exchanged glances that had him muttering under his breath. Mostly because they were right. Something about Audra Marshall called to him. A reaction that had him wanting to pull back. Away. To steer clear of the feelings she and her children stirred in him. He would not place himself in the same emotionally vulnerable position Nathan had. Would not allow himself to care too much.

Chapter Five

Audra stood looking out across the moonlit yard from her bedroom window. It was only seven fifteen in the evening, but after the day she'd put in working on the house she should be every bit as tired as her children, who had gone to bed early. Actually, she was—physically. But her mind refused to shut down. It was awhirl with all the things that still needed to be done. That list seemed to grow every day, weighing down on her to the point she felt as if she were suffocating at times. It was at those moments she prayed for strength and did her best to focus on all she had managed to accomplish in just under a week.

She'd polished all the wood trim until her arms ached, giving the house a clean, lemony scent. Then she'd painted the kitchen a soft buttery yellow that brought life and light to the room. The hallway and living room walls were coated in a shade she'd chosen called warmed biscuit, which felt cozy and welcoming. A huge change from the long since abandoned feel the house once had. In addition to the new paint, curtains she'd brought from her house in Chicago hung in several of the rooms, having needed only a bit of their length taken off. Those were the positive results of her hard work.

The negatives, of which there were plenty, were a leaking kitchen sink, which she had tried to repair but only made worse, creaking floorboards in the living room, which she had pulled up only to reveal a large area of rotted flooring underneath, and crooked shutters too high for her to reach safely. The list went on and on.

With a sigh, she let her gaze travel across the moonlit yard to settle onto the not-so-white picket fence that lined the front of her property. It had been barely visible from the house before Carter had shown up alongside his brother, trimming the wildly overgrown hedges while Logan mowed the yard. That had been three days before, a day after they'd helped move all her belongings from the moving containers to the house. Somehow, it felt like much longer.

While both Nathan and Logan had stopped

by that week to see if she needed anything, she hadn't seen or heard from Carter since he'd trimmed back her hedges. Even then, they hadn't had much of a chance to talk as he'd rushed off as soon as the job was finished. She knew she shouldn't take it personally. Carter was a busy man with a business to run. But so were his brothers and they had found the time to check on her, she reminded herself, feeling an unexpected note of hurt.

Had she done something to offend Carter? Audra searched her memory for anything she might have said that would have put him off, but she could come up with nothing. Other than her refusal to hire him to take care of her house's much-needed renovations. Was it possible that his and Nathan's company was in financial need? She'd never given that possibility any thought.

What she did know now was that she'd been far too confident in her ability to read how-to books on home repair and then apply what she'd learned to her own house. How wrong she'd been to think she could handle a job this big on her own.

Her cell phone rang out behind her, startling Audra from her troubled thoughts. Turning away from the window, she crossed the room and grabbed the phone from her nightstand.

Not recognizing the number on her cell phone's caller ID screen, she said, "Hello?"

"Ms. Marshall, this is Rachel Johns. Reverend Johns's wife. We spoke a couple of days ago when you stopped by to inquire about the secretarial/bookkeeping job we have advertised in the paper."

"Yes," Audra said with forced calm, trying not to get her hopes up.

"I'm sorry to be calling so late in the evening, but I told you we'd get back to you by today and didn't want you to be left wondering. The reverend and I have been out most of the day making hospital calls and paying home visits to some of our under-the-weather parishioners, or I would have tried to reach you sooner."

"It's quite all right," she assured the older woman. "In fact, your timing is perfect. I just tucked my children into their beds for the night, so I'm free to talk without any interruption."

"Well, I won't keep you on long. As a mother myself, I know how precious those moments of solitude can be, no matter how much we adore our little ones. Not that mine are little anymore. They're all grown up with lives of their own, but I do remember those days."

Audra smiled. Sometimes the peace and quiet was nice. Especially after the past few days of trying to make the house livable.

"Anyway," the reverend's wife continued, "we'd like to offer you the job if you haven't already found another. It's thirty-five hours a week with an hour for lunch. And, as we discussed the other day, the pay isn't much over minimum wage, but you'd have health insurance with reasonably priced add-ons for your children if you're interested."

A huge worry lifted from her shoulders at those words. "I would definitely be interested."

"I know you're new in town and you mentioned having no family, so feel free to bring your children in with you whenever needed. They can entertain themselves in the children's playroom while you work."

"I really appreciate that," she told her. "At least, until I can find someone to help me with child care when needed. Would it be possible for me to take my lunch break later in the afternoon, so I can use that time to pick them up from school? I'm hoping to get them enrolled as soon as possible."

The older woman nodded. "That would be fine. Take your hour lunch break whenever you need it. We have an answering machine here that can pick up when you're out of the office and you can return any calls when you return to work."

Could she have found a more perfect job for

her situation? *Oh, Heavenly Father, thank You for this wonderfully timed blessing.* "I would love very much to accept the position."

"That's wonderful news. My husband will be so happy to hear it. I have to admit that if we hadn't already been thoroughly impressed with you after our visit the other day, Carter Cooper's kind words on your behalf would have swayed our decision greatly in your favor."

"Carter talked to you about me?" she said in surprise.

"Not exactly," the woman explained. "We overheard him in the hardware store telling Mr. Anderson—he's the store's owner—to treat you right when you came in for supplies. He said you were a single mother trying to do right by your children. And that you have a tender heart and a kind smile, and more pluck than most of the men he knows."

"He said all that?" she gasped, her cheeks warming at such unexpected compliments.

"He most certainly did. Apparently, you've made quite an impression on that young man."

The reverend's wife had no idea. Having had to come to her rescue multiple times since meeting her, she could only imagine what Carter Cooper's impression of her must be. But he'd been kind in his words and for that she was grateful. But what thrilled her most was his comment about her having pluck. She'd gone so many years without any real backbone when her children had needed her to have one. But she'd been trying so hard to be a good Christian. What she hadn't been able to separate at the time was the difference between being a good Christian and being a floor mat for her ex-husband. In the end, she'd had no choice but to toughen up, using that pluck Carter had mentioned to get both she and her children out of an emotionally harmful situation.

"It's late," Rachel said on the other end of the line, pulling Audra from her thoughts. "Why don't you swing by sometime this week to pick up some paperwork I'll need you to fill out before you start? I can answer any more questions you might have then."

"That sounds good to me."

"Good. How about we set your start date for the Monday after next? It'll give you some time to settle into your new home."

"That would be perfect," Audra told her. "Tomorrow, I'm going to see about getting Mason and Lily enrolled into school here. I'll swing by and pick up those papers while I'm out."

"See you tomorrow, then," the reverend's wife replied.

Audra pressed End on her phone screen and fought the urge to let out a whoop of excitement. The children had played hard that day. The last thing she wanted to do was wake them. But she could barely contain her excitement. Extra income *and* health coverage. Now all she had to do was admit defeat where her house renovations were concerned and then do something about it.

"Mommy…"

Audra turned to find her daughter standing in the doorway. "Sweetie, what are you doing out of bed?"

Her daughter rubbed her sleep-filled eyes as she looked up at her. "I had a bad dream. Did you have one, too?"

Audra knelt in front of her little girl. "No, honey. Mommy just has a lot on her mind and it's making it hard for me to sleep." Reaching out, she brushed her daughter's fine, silky hair away from her tiny face. "Would you like to tell me about your bad dream?"

Her daughter hesitated before lowering her gaze to the floor and shaking her head.

"Talking about it might make you feel better," she told her. "And sharing your fears with someone else can sometimes help to chase them far away."

Lily looked up at her once more, biting at her bottom lip as Audra sometimes did when she was troubled over something. "Can I sleep in your bed tonight?"

She smiled down at her daughter. "If you promise not to take all the covers."

"I promise."

Audra stood and lifted Lily into her arms, carrying her over to the bed. Lowering her atop the turned-down sheets, she lovingly tucked her daughter in. Then, with a worried sigh, she settled down onto the edge of the mattress. "Did you have a bad dream about snakes?" she asked, having had one or two herself since their run-in with that huge rat snake in the backyard.

Lily shook her head. "No. I dreamed that we moved away."

"To another house?" she said, certain that her children would be thrilled to live anywhere but in the old, dilapidated house Audra had chosen for them. But if that were so, her daughter's dream wouldn't have been a bad one.

"No," she said with a sleepy pout. "We moved far away from Braxton and our new house."

Lily's reply took her by surprise. "You *like* living in this big old house?"

Her daughter nodded.

Thank You, Lord, for that small blessing. It would break her heart to know her children were so unhappy with their new home they were having nightmares about it. "I'm glad you're happy here. And I promise to make our house a very warm, wonderful place to live in. It's just going to take Mommy a little time to get everything done."

"So we won't have to move again?" Lily said almost anxiously.

"I have no plans to," she told her with a reassuring smile.

"Good, 'cause I like playing with Katie," she said sleepily. "And I like Carter."

"Mr. Cooper," Audra promptly amended.

"Mr. Cooper," Lily mumbled softly. "Even if he doesn't like us anymore."

"Why would you think he doesn't like us?" Audra asked, her brows knitting in concern.

Lily yawned, her eyes closing. "Because he doesn't come see us anymore…" Her daughter's words drifted off as she settled into sleep, but they remained firm in Audra's mind long into the night.

"How are things coming along out at Ms. Marshall's place?" Nathan asked as he stepped from the kitchen, placing the pot of chili he'd made for that night's dinner onto the table. Katie followed behind with a basket of corn bread.

"Couldn't say," Carter mumbled, feeling

that ever-present tug of guilt he had when it came to Audra Marshall and her two children. Guilt he was forever trying to convince himself he shouldn't be feeling. After all, he'd rescued her from her porch roof, helped move all her belongings into her new house, replaced her back door and trimmed all of her hedges. Surely, he'd fulfilled his Christian duty. Or so he kept trying to convince himself. If that were so, why then did it feel as though he'd abandoned her?

"You haven't talked to her lately?" Logan said with a frown.

"I've been busy," he muttered as he buttered himself a slice of the still oven-warm corn bread.

"Busy avoiding her," Nathan said as he scooped a spoonful of chili from the pot and dumped it into his bowl.

"Are you mad at her, Uncle Carter?" Katie asked worriedly from where she sat across the table from him.

He shot his brothers a scowl for even bringing the conversation up around Katie. "No, Katydid," he told her with a gentle smile. "I'm not mad at Ms. Marshall. Your daddy and I have been very busy with work and that takes up most of my time."

"But Daddy and me had time to go see her."

Carter's gaze snapped in his older brother's direction.

Nathan grinned. "Figured somebody ought to swing by and see how things were going."

"I figured the same thing," Logan admitted.

Carter's head swiveled sharply to where his younger brother sat at the other end of the table. "You went to see her, too?"

Logan chuckled as he reached for the salt-shaker. "Careful, Carter. You're sounding a little territorial for a woman you claim to have washed your hands of."

"Washed his hands of?" Katie repeated, her tiny brows drawn together in confusion.

"How about we eat dinner before it gets cold?" Carter suggested, his irritation barely contained. He should have been the one looking in on Audra. Not his brothers. But that day she'd offered to make him and Logan grilled cheese sandwiches when they'd finished working on the yard, she'd sent him running. His momma used to make him grilled cheese sandwiches when he was a little boy and then well into adulthood, knowing they were a favorite of his. It was a reminder of what he'd lost. It was also a reminder of what he risked by getting close to Audra and her children. A risk he wasn't willing to take.

No sooner had that last thought crossed his mind than his cell phone set to ringing, bringing all conversation to a halt. "Sorry," he apologized as he pulled the phone from his jeans pocket. Normally, he set it on vibrate during family meals, as did his brothers, but that night he'd forgotten to switch it over. A glance at the lit screen showed a number with an area code he wasn't familiar with. "Probably a wrong number," he said as he brought the phone to his ear. "Carter Cooper speaking."

"Carter…" the soft, very feminine voice on the other end of the line said.

"Audra?"

"I hope I'm not catching you at a bad time." She sounded anxious.

"No," he replied, ignoring his family's curious stares. "Is everything okay?"

"Yes and no."

Well, that helped to ease his concern. With a frown, he asked, "Is it one of the children?"

"Lily and Mason are fine," she assured him. "But thank you for caring enough to ask."

His caring about them was the problem. He didn't want to care at the level he did. Had done his best to squash those warm-and-fuzzy, care-too-much thoughts Audra and her children stirred in him.

"I'm calling because…" she began and then hesitated for a long moment. Finally, she said, "Well, because I need you."

Run! The grilled cheese was nothing when compared to those last three little words. *I need you.*

"I know it's last-minute," she continued, "but you were right."

"I was?" He had no idea what he'd been right about. All his mind could focus on was that softly spoken *I need you.*

"I can't do the renovations on my own. I'd like to hire you if you have the time to fit the work into your schedule."

It took a moment for her words to sink in. "You're calling to hire me?" Not to tell him that she'd noticed his absence in her life. One that had been intentional on his part. So why then, when it was what he'd wanted, did it bother him that she hadn't missed him? Maybe because he'd found himself missing her. Missing them. How had that happened when their paths had only crossed for the first time barely a week ago?

"I know what I said," she admitted with a sigh. "But I have discovered that I'm a much better homemaker than home repairer. Far better suited to being a mother to my children. That includes having the ability to throw impromptu tea parties for dolls, to make paper airplanes that actually fly, to bake the best chocolate chip cookies around and to teach them what it means to love and be loved."

To be loved. They deserved that. *She* deserved that. Carter cleared the unwanted emotion from his throat. "Admirable skills to have," he said, meaning it wholeheartedly.

"Did I mention that I'm far less suited for plumbing issues? And that my living room floor has a hole in it?"

That got his attention. "A hole?" he asked, straightening in his chair.

Around the table, his entire family was hanging on to his every word. Even little Katie was staring up at him in wide-eyed silence. A rarity for his little chatterbox of a niece.

"The floor was making such loud, creaking noises," Audra explained, "that I decided to glue the loose boards down. Only when I managed to get a few of the squeaky boards pulled up, I discovered the flooring beneath it is slightly rotted."

The thought of that weak flooring giving way and Audra or one of her young children accidentally slipping through to the unfinished basement below had him cringing. "Steer clear of that room," he said firmly. "I'll be there first thing in the morning to have a look at it. What's wrong with your plumbing?"

She hesitated and then admitted, "I attempted to repair a leak under the kitchen sink and now it's really dripping."

"Do you need me to come over tonight?" he asked with a worried frown.

"Tomorrow is fine," she assured him. "I placed a bucket under the pipe and have a spare to switch out when it gets too full."

From the sound of things, she really did need him. Or, at least, she needed his help. "Whatever you do," he told her, "don't attempt to fix anything else."

Her lilting laughter filled his ear. "I promise you have no worry there. I'm hanging up my home-repair hat. Well, except for the small tasks like painting."

He was more than glad to hear it. "Then I can sleep easy tonight," he said with a grin.

"One more thing…" she began.

"Don't tell me you tried to do roof repairs."

"Not a chance," she replied, much to his relief. "I was wondering if you might be able to give me an estimate, so I'll have an idea of what I'm getting into financially."

"Once I have a look around, I can do that. But I promise it's gonna be lower than any other contractor in these parts can offer. You pay for the materials. I'll take care of the labor."

"I can't let you do that."

"It's that or nothing," he said, digging in his heels.

"Carter…"

"Audra…"

"Fine, but only if you allow me to make you some home-cooked meals whenever you're here working."

He could almost envision the stubborn tilt of her chin at that moment. "That's not necessary."

"If you're going to work on my house without charging me for it, the least I can do is feed you," she told him. "And in case you were wondering, my cooking skills far surpass my plumbing skills."

That had him chuckling. "Reckon we'll work well together, because I know how to plumb, but my cooking leaves something to be desired."

"Then don't eat before you come over in the morning. I'm making waffles for breakfast."

"I look forward to it. See you in the morning."

"See you in the morning."

He ended the call and shoved his phone back into his jeans pocket. A glance around the dinner table revealed three faces staring his way. "What?"

"What?" Logan repeated. "Are you serious? You get a call from the very woman you've been avoiding all week and went from a look of panic to concern to grinning from ear to ear all in one short phone call. Care to fill us in on what's going on?"

"Why were you avoiding Ms. Marshall?" Katie asked with a frown. Of course, those would be the words she'd latch on to.

"Not avoiding," he told her. "I've been busy."

"Fortunately for Ms. Marshall," Nathan said, "Uncle Carter's busy schedule suddenly seems to have freed up."

"She pulled up some of the hardwood planking in the living room and discovered the subfloor is rotted."

His older brother frowned. "I was worried that might be the case as much give as it had when we carried her furniture in."

"Pretty safe bet the whole subfloor's in need of replacing," Logan muttered around the bite of buttered corn bread he'd just taken.

Carter nodded.

"I don't want them to fall through the floor like I did," Katie blurted out, her dark eyes wide with worry.

Nathan lifted her off the chair and settled her

onto his lap. "They're not gonna," he said quietly. "There is no storm. And Uncle Carter is gonna make sure to keep them safe."

Keep them safe. Just as he had promised Isabel he would do for Nathan and Katie.

Her tiny head shifted, her dark eyes looking up at Carter. "Will you, Uncle Carter?"

"I will."

"Promise?"

"Promise." For a man determined to avoid any sort of emotional commitment, at least beyond what he had with his family, he was sure piling on the responsibility, promising to keep someone else he cared about safe from harm. And there was no denying that he cared about Audra Marshall and her two young children. Thankfully, his responsibility toward Audra and her children would only last as long as the renovations. Once they'd been completed, giving them a safe place to start their new lives, he'd be able to put a little distance between himself and the woman who had his thoughts and emotions all in a tangle.

Carter looked to Nathan. "I'm not sure what I'll be getting into tomorrow morning."

"Not a problem," his older brother replied. "The crew and I can handle things at the site. We're ready to start wrapping the job up anyway. You do what you need to do to assure Audra and the kids are safe."

He nodded. "Appreciate it."

"Can I go to Lily and Mason's with you, Uncle Carter?" Katie asked, her dark eyes pleading.

He offered a tender smile. "Afraid not, Katy-did. You've got school tomorrow."

Her lips formed a pout. "Mason and Lily don't have to go to school."

"They will," he told her. "Once their momma has a chance to get them signed up for school here."

"If you need any help out there," Logan said, "I'm free the day after tomorrow."

Carter nodded. "I'll keep that in mind."

"Same goes for me," Nathan said. "I could run out in the evenings to lend a hand if need be."

His niece clapped excitedly. "Me, too!"

"Tell you what. How about I see what I'm getting into first?" Carter said. "Then we'll see what sort of help I'll be needing."

His brothers nodded and went back to eating. However, Katie still had her gaze pinned on him.

"Something wrong, Katydid?"

She hemmed and hawed for a moment and then said, "Be sure to make their house real pretty so they'll wanna stay here. Lily says her mommy likes red flowers."

He chuckled. "Flowers and making places pretty are your uncle Logan's specialty." Yet he found himself storing that little tidbit of information away. Even if he was quite certain he'd never have need of it.

Chapter Six

❧

"Carter!" Lily exclaimed as she and Mason ran out of the house to greet him.

"Mr. Cooper," Audra said, correcting her daughter as she followed after them.

The kids wrapped themselves around his long legs like the hardiest of vines, smiling up at him. Their response to his arrival had him chuckling.

"Kids," Audra said, the flush of what he could only assume was embarrassment flooding her cheeks. Not that she had any reason to be embarrassed.

"They're okay," he assured her with a grin. Then he looked down at her children. "Step on my boots and hold on tight."

What was she doing? She didn't have to wait long to find out as Carter Cooper, large hands braced on her children's backs, started once more for the house. Her children, giggling in delight, clung to his jean-clad legs as he moved.

Such a silly thing, yet it delighted her children to no end.

"Morning," he greeted with a smile as he stepped up onto the porch with his tiny hitch-hikers firmly attached.

She returned the smile. "Morning."

"Brought you a special delivery," he teased. "A pair of candlesticks for the mantel."

Mason snickered. Lily squealed. "We're not candlesticks. We're people."

"Kids who aren't going to be having waffles for breakfast if we don't get back to making them," Audra said, laughing softly as both her children pushed away from Carter and ran inside. The old screen door banged shut behind them. Turning to Carter with an apologetic smile, she said, "I'm so sorry about the ambush. That's the last thing I expected from them. My children are usually pretty standoffish when it comes to men." She paused, then amended, "Well, except for when it comes to you, it seems."

He flashed a crooked grin. "No need to apologize. It's nice having someone, or in this case two little someones, excited to see me."

Three, she wanted to say. Thankfully, she refrained from adding herself to that list. She was not about to complicate her life any more than it already was. Especially when that complication came in the form of a tall, dark and handsome Texan. One with the most knee-weakening smile she had ever seen.

"Besides," he continued, "Mason and Lily aren't to blame for their enthusiastic greeting. I am."

"You are?" she replied with a curious tilt of her head. "How do you figure that?" Hadn't it been her children who had charged out of the house like a stampeding herd of cattle, practically mowing him down in their excitement to see him?

"They couldn't help themselves," he told her. "You see, dogs and kids can't seem to resist my charm."

"And every woman in the county, no doubt," she replied, intending the remark to be teasing. But his playful expression changed and she found herself wishing she could pull the words back.

"Seeing as how I'm not looking for anything long-term, I try and keep my charm securely under wraps when it comes to husband-hunting females."

His response should have given her a sense of relief. She was anything but a husband-hunting female. In fact, a husband was the last thing she wanted or needed in her life. But she couldn't help but wonder why he felt the way he did. "Another reason we'll work well together as a team," she told him with a soft smile. "I'm not looking for anything long-term, either. Not even short-term. So there's no chance of any sort of messy emotional entanglements getting in the way of our business arrangement."

He nodded in agreement.

She reached for the door. "Hope you brought an appetite. We made double the waffle batter."

He chuckled. "I think I can hold my own."

She led him inside, pausing when she realized he wasn't following her to the kitchen. Turning, she found him looking into the living room with a frown and she knew why. "I can explain…"

He glanced her way, all humor gone from his face. "When we spoke on the phone you said you had only pulled up a few of the floorboards."

"I had. Then I went in and pulled up a couple more to see if the floor was bad in other places."

"What part of 'steer clear of this room' did I fail to get across to you last night?"

"I was careful," she said in her own defense. "I only removed a board or two here and there to get a better idea of what I was going to be getting into."

He dragged a hand down over his tanned face with a heavy sigh as if struggling for patience. "Look," he said with forced calm, "these floors are old and, as you've already seen, unsafe in places. Please, Audra, let me do what I do best."

"Mommy," Lily whined from the kitchen doorway, drawing both their gazes her way. "We're hungry."

She glanced up at Carter. "Looks like it's time for me to do what I do best."

Fifteen minutes later, Carter was seated at the breakfast table, feasting on the best waffles he'd ever tasted. And that was saying a lot, because his momma had been a mighty fine cook.

"We get to go to church with Mommy," Lily announced before shoving a syrup-covered fingertip into her mouth.

"Then I'll be seeing you there," he said, meeting Audra's gaze across the table.

"I think my daughter's referring to my new job," she replied, lowering her gaze as she stabbed at another bite of waffle. "But we'll be attending worship on Sundays, as well."

"Job?" he repeated.

"Mommy's going to be working for God," Mason explained.

Audra laughed softly. "I suppose in a way I am. I've been hired on as the church's secretary and will be handling bookkeeping duties, as well. In fact, we're running into town this afternoon to get Mason enrolled in school and see if we can get Lily into a preschool class. If not, Mrs. Johns said I can bring Lily in with me and she can entertain herself in the playroom while I work."

"Me, too!" Mason exclaimed.

Audra smile at him. "Yes, Mason, too, if he has a day off school that I have to work."

"Sounds like the perfect job for you," Carter told her.

"My prayers have been answered," she said, meeting his gaze. "More than once this past week, truth be told."

"You're not the only one whose prayers were answered this week," he admitted as he plucked up a crispy strip of bacon and bit into it. "When I saw you up on that there roof…" He shook his head, letting the rest of his statement go unsaid.

"I prayed you would come back," Lily chirped, looking up at him with her brightest smile, one nearly identical to her mother's.

Carter looked down at her, his guarded heart melting just a little. "That was mighty nice of you to think of me in your prayers. And here I am."

"Praying never worked with our daddy," Mason grumbled into his orange juice. "He didn't like being around us."

What did one say to that? From what Audra had told him, it was the truth. His jaw clenched in anger at what this man had done to his children emotionally. "Well, I like being around you."

Mason glanced up. "Then why did you stay away so long?"

Though it had only been days, he knew to a child it could seem like forever. Before Carter could respond, Audra said, "Honey, Mr. Cooper has a construction company to run. He doesn't have a lot of free time."

Guilt dug its claws deep into his conscience. He had time to spare. His not stopping by had been his attempt to push Audra from his thoughts. It hadn't worked. And in the process, he'd made a young boy feel abandoned—again. "The schedule's lightening up some. How about I take a look at things around the place for your mom and fix her sink and then afterward maybe we could play a little ball?"

Mason shrugged, his gaze pinned to his plate. "I'm not very good at it."

"Neither was I at your age," Carter told him.

"But I got better. I just had to practice a little more. So what do you say? Wanna throw the ball around later?"

A soft sniffle drew his gaze back to Audra, who immediately shot to her feet and walked over to the sink carrying her plate and half-empty juice glass.

"Can I, Mommy?" Mason called out to her.

She reached out, her back to them, and turned on the sink to rinse off her plate. "If Mr. Carter's sure he has time," she said, her voice catching.

Carter watched her worriedly. The slight shudder in her shoulders had him wanting to push out of his chair and go over to her. "I wouldn't have made the offer if I didn't have the time to spare." Had he said something to upset her?

"I like to dance," Lily announced. "Do you know how to dance?"

"He's not a girl," her brother replied.

Carter dragged his troubled gaze from Audra to focus on her children. "Dancing isn't just for girls," he told Mason and then turned to Lily. "I've danced with Katydid a few times, but I bet I'm nowhere near as good as you and my niece are. How about you teach me a few dance moves after Mason and I finish playing catch?"

He certainly didn't want her to feel like he was leaving her out.

"Okay!"

"Kids," Audra called out without turning, "why don't you bring your dishes over to the sink? Then you can go upstairs and brush your teeth."

They did as their mother asked, quickly gathering up their empty plates, forks and juice glasses and carrying them over to where Audra was still scrubbing away at her own plate. One that looked plenty clean to him, which had him frowning in concern once more.

When the children scurried from the room, smiles on their faces, Carter pushed away from the table and stood, intending to collect his dishes and carry them over to the sink.

"You can leave your dishes," Audra said over her shoulder. "I'll see to them."

"You already fed me," he told her as he crossed the room. "Least I can do is help with the cleanup." He reached past her to lower his plate into the sudsy water. His glass and fork followed. "Audra…" he said as she continued looking down at the plate in her hands.

"Yes?" she replied with a slight tremor in her voice.

He couldn't take it. The knowledge that he might have unintentionally said or done something to make her cry. With a sigh, he reached out, took the plate she had been rinsing off and set it on the counter, and then gently turned her to face him. Sure enough, tears shimmered, unshed, in her beautiful eyes. "Wanna talk about it?"

She sniffed softly. "And turn on the real waterworks?" Shaking her head, she said with a half sob, "I can't."

"You can," he said softly. "I promise I'm a good listener."

She searched his concerned gaze as if questioning the sincerity of his words. "I thought that men preferred to avoid a woman's tears," she said, her bottom lip trembling.

It was clear she was struggling to hold back those aforementioned tears. "For the most part," he admitted honestly. "But there are times when tears have just gotta happen."

She groaned as if in pain. "If I allow myself to break down now, I'm afraid I might keep on breaking until there's nothing left of me. I need to be strong—for my children," she said on a broken sob.

Her words tore at his heart. He pulled her close, folding his arms around her in a comforting embrace as she buried her face in his shirt. "Let me be strong for you, darlin'," he told her, his own words close to breaking.

Warm tears soaked through the cotton of his T-shirt.

"If it was something I said or did…" he said, gently running a hand up and down her trembling back. He wanted desperately to fix whatever it was that had set her off. Because that's what he did. He fixed things.

Her head lifted, her cheeks damp with tears. "You didn't do anything. Yet," she added with a sniffle, "you did everything."

He lifted a dark brow. "Darlin', I'm a man. We need answers plain and simply put. We're not real good at trying to read between the lines."

She managed a smile that lightened the heaviness that had fallen over his heart. Then she pushed away from him, scrubbing the tears from her cheeks. Carter wanted to draw her back into his arms. Wanted to hold her until he knew everything was all right. But he held back, letting his hands fall to his sides.

Audra glanced out the window and then back up at him. "My children used to beg their father to play with them. Anything from coloring in books to pushing them in a swing in our backyard. Bradford would always send them away, telling them he didn't have time for ridiculous child's play." Tears shimmered in her eyes. "And here you are, a man who barely knows my children, a man who so generously offered to fit our home repairs into your own busy schedule, and yet you offer to play catch with my son, and…" She burst into another round of sobs, choking out, "…even dance with my daughter."

His initial thought to her admission was relief that he hadn't been the one to cause her tears. Then anger followed. Anger on behalf of her children who had longed for their father's love and attention only to be pushed aside time and time again.

Reaching out, he swiped a trail of tears away from her damp cheek with his thumb. "I'm real sorry you had to live that way. That Mason and Lily had to live that way. You all deserved so much more than you were given. Unlike your ex, I don't have any issues with joining in child's play. Katie always has me playing something that most grown men would feel a little silly doing, but I treasure every moment of it."

Her expression was one of surprise and then softened. "You're a very special man, Carter Cooper. Katie is very blessed to have you in her life."

"No," he replied. "We're the ones who are blessed. After nearly losing her in the tornado that struck Braxton a while back, my brothers and I all have a whole new appreciation for life and for family."

"The same storm she lost her mother in?" she asked.

He met her searching gaze. "She told you?" Katie rarely spoke about what had happened that day. The fact that she felt comfortable enough to bring up her painful past with Audra spoke volumes.

She nodded.

"We lost our folks that day, as well," he admitted, trying to tamp down the grief that threatened to surface.

"Oh, Carter," she groaned, reaching out to place a comforting hand on his arm. "I can't imagine how hard that must have been for all of you."

"Still is," he heard himself admitting. "Especially for Nathan."

"I don't know how he does it. Going on after such a devastating loss."

"He does it for Katie. Just as you've gone on for the sake of your children."

She nodded. "Faith has played a large part in giving me the strength to go on."

The sound of water spilling out onto the floor cut their conversation short, drawing both of their gazes downward.

Audra shrieked, reaching out to turn off the

water that had been left running in the sink when he'd turned her to him. "The bucket!"

"Bucket?" he repeated as he bent to open the cupboard door below the right side of the kitchen sink. Inside, a white plastic bucket was filled to the top, the excess water draining over the bucket's edge. Kneeling on the wet floor, he glanced up to do a visual inspection of the old copper plumbing above where water had finally stopped draining from the small split in one of the copper pipes.

"Bad?" Audra asked as she peered over his shoulder.

"Looks like we'll be starting with the kitchen sink today," he said in response. "There's a small crack in the copper piping."

"Doesn't sound like a simple fix," she said with a sigh.

He glanced back at her. "The good news is it's fixable and the rest of the copper piping under here still looks pretty solid. At some point, you might want to consider replacing it, though. Do you have an extra bucket or pan I could switch this bucket out with?"

"In the pantry," she replied. "Be right back." She returned a few moments later, handing it over to him. "I'll take that one," she said, motioning past him to the filled bucket.

Carter switched them out and then stood,

carefully hefting the water-filled bucket. "It's heavy. I'll get it. You might wanna see to that water on the floor while I go dump this."

Grabbing a couple of dish towels from a nearby drawer, she knelt where he had been and began soaking up the overflow on the floor and inside of the sink cupboard.

He stepped out onto the back porch, needing a moment away to collect himself. The emotional strife Audra had been forced to deal with during her marriage had him wanting to pull her into his arms again. At the same time, he was ready to get in his truck and head north in search of her ex with the intention of having a little chat with the coldhearted man. Unfortunately, he could do neither. Audra wasn't his to hold. And her ex, well, the Lord would see to him. What he could do was be there for her children, giving them at least a small example of what it meant to have a man who cared and wanted to spend time with them in their life.

Audra tried to keep from smiling as she drove into town. Despite the emotional outburst she'd had that morning in the kitchen, she felt better than she had in a very long time. Carter had done that for her. Not only by being there for her when she most needed it, but also for his being there for her children. Seeing him with her son as he taught Mason how to throw a curveball, and then afterward with her daughter, who had at some point decided that today's special dance was going to be ballet, was a moment she would always hold dear in her heart.

Carter hadn't balked at her daughter's request. Not even for a second. He'd simply smiled, then kicked off his boots so he could rise up on his toes like a true ballerina, following her daughter's every instruction. Lily had giggled so joyously it had brought tears of happiness to Audra's eyes. Even Mason had joined in, mimicking Carter's poorly done pirouettes until her son collapsed onto the grass in a fit of uncontrollable laughter.

To think she'd been so eager to push Carter away that first day. Thankfully, for her and her children, he was a determinedly stubborn man. God had brought Cooper into their lives for a reason. Aside from rescuing her from the roof. Maybe He'd sent Cooper there to show her children that real men didn't mind spending time with their kids and weren't afraid to show emotion. Real men built others up instead of tearing them down.

She thought back to the life she'd had when she was married to Bradford. Never having a say over anything. Not with the house. Not with the finances. Not with her children. He'd taken nearly all control away from her and she'd foolishly allowed it. But not any longer. This was her life and she was going to have the control in the way she lived it. The way her beloved children lived theirs.

"Is this going to take long?" Mason called from the backseat of the minivan. "Mr. Cooper might need my help."

More like her son wanted to get back to the house to help Carter. "I think he's perfectly capable of handling things on his own while we get you signed up for school."

"Me, too!" her daughter squeaked from where she sat buckled in the second-row passenger-side seat.

"You, too," Audra replied with a smile as she caught her daughter's reflection in the rearview mirror. Returning her gaze to the road ahead, she said, "As long as one of their preschool classes has an opening. Remember what Mommy told you this morning. We're late signing you up, so we might not be able to get you into a class right now. If that happens, you can come to work with me while Mason is in school."

She turned into the church parking lot and pulled into one of the empty spaces closest to the main door. "Everyone unbuckle. Mommy has to pick up some paperwork from Mrs. Johns before we run by the school."

No sooner had they stepped into the building than they were greeted by Reverend Johns. "Well, look who we have here."

Audra smiled. "I was just stopping by to pick up that paperwork your wife needs me to fill out before I start working next week."

He nodded. "Rachel mentioned you'd be coming by. She's in the office. I'm on my way out to visit one of our parishioners who's scheduled for open-heart surgery tomorrow morning." He smiled as his gaze took in her children. "Hope to see you three at the service on Sunday."

"We'll be there," she assured him. Getting involved in church again was very important to her. Her decision to divorce Bradford had filled her with overwhelming guilt over her failure to save the holy union they had entered into, turning her back on the commitment she'd made to God that day to love, honor and obey her husband until death do them part. That guilt, despite knowing it was Bradford who essentially walked away from the marriage, and shame at letting God down, had her attending Sunday services back in Chicago less and less. But she wanted to find herself back in God's good graces again, here where she intended to make a new start. He must want that, as well. Why else would the only job listing locally be for the position at Braxton's only church? If that wasn't a sign from above, she didn't know what was.

He nodded, seemingly pleased by her reply. "Will you be entering Braxton's annual pie bake-off next month?" he asked.

"Pie bake-off?"

"I like pie!" Lily exclaimed beside her.

The reverend chuckled. "It's being held two Sundays from next. Every year, the funds raised go to a need the town has. This year it's going toward rebuilding the community center. We lost it in a tornado the Christmas before last."

"Mommy can bake a pie!" Mason said excitedly.

"A really, really good pie," Lily agreed, rubbing her tummy. "And sometimes we get to help her."

Audra's smile returned with their unrestrained exuberance. It was true. She did love to bake. Especially desserts. "So it's not too late to enter?" she asked, finding herself eager to contribute to the town's fund-raising efforts.

"Not at all," he replied. "I believe they're accepting entrants up until the start of judging. And being one of the judges, one with a very sweet tooth," he added with a grin, "I would more than welcome another pie to taste."

"Will you do it?" Mason asked, looking up at her.

"Please, Mommy," Lily added, bouncing up and down on her toes.

Audra laughed, turning her attention back to the reverend. "Looks like you're going to have another pie to taste."

"Wonderful!' he said, his friendly smile widening. "Be sure to let Rachel know and she'll add your name to the sign-up sheet."

"I will."

"See you Sunday," he said with a wave as he continued on toward the door that led to the parking lot.

Rachel Johns poked her head out from the church office. "I thought I heard voices out here. Come on back," she said, waving them in her direction.

Audra herded her children down the hall with a smile. "I hope we're not catching you at a bad time."

"Not at all," Rachel replied, motioning them into the room. "I have your papers right over here." She crossed the room, reaching for a manila envelope lying atop her desk. Handing it over to Audra, she said, "Take a few days to read through these and fill them out. If you could get them back to me by Friday, that would be wonderful."

"I will. Thank you." She clutched the envelope to her blouse. Inside was an answer to her prayers. At least, one of them. Health-care coverage for her family.

Lily gave Audra's shirt an impatient tug. "Don't forget to ask her," her daughter whispered beside her. Not that whispering did much good in an office that small.

Rachel tempered a grin as she waited for whatever it was Audra had to ask her.

"Sorry," she apologized. "A little too much sugar this morning."

"We had homemade waffles," Mason announced.

Lily nodded. "With bunches of syrup."

"The only way to eat waffles," the older woman said, clearly charmed, and then turned to Audra.

"Reverend Johns mentioned the pie bake-off in a few weeks. We were hoping to sign up for it."

"The entry fee is fifteen dollars," she said, somewhat hesitantly.

While she was trying to be careful financially, and Rachel knew it, this was for a good cause. Not to mention a small way to contribute to the town they now called home. "When would you need my entry fee?"

"The day of the judging is fine." She walked

around the desk and withdrew a yellow sheet
of paper from one of the side drawers. "Whenever is best for you. Here's a list of rules for the
competition. Fill out the entry form slip at the
bottom and give it, along with the entry fee, to
Mrs. Danner when you arrive that afternoon.
She's in charge this year."

Audra glanced down at the brightly colored
paper she held in her hands. The judging was
scheduled to begin at 3:00 p.m., which gave
her plenty of time to get home from church,
fix the children and Carter lunch and then get
to baking. Lifting her gaze, she smiled. "I…"
she began and then looked to her children. "*We*
are looking forward to joining in."

Her children beamed at being included, their
happiness over something so simple warming
her heart.

The older woman smiled. "Well, we look forward to having the three of you be a part of the
fund-raiser. Oh, and I almost forgot to mention
that the remainder of the contest pies, once our
judges have tasted their slices and chosen a
winner, will be auctioned off to the highest bid-
der." She fluttered her hand in the air. "It's all
on the entry form entrant information sheet."

Now the pressure was really on. Not only
would a handful of judges be tasting her baking for the competition, but someone was also

going to be paying hard-earned money for the remainder of her pie.

The front door to Audra's house swung open, thudding against the wall. "We're home!" Lily's tiny voice called out from the front entryway.

Carter set down the crowbar he'd been using to pull up the wood planks in the living room and then sat back on his heels, wiping the sweat from his brow with the back of his sleeve. "I'm in here," he called back with a smile. "But don't come into the room," he added in warning. "I lifted a big chunk of the floor while you were away and don't want anyone getting hurt."

Mason voice followed as he joined his sister inside. "Did you tell him yet?" he asked excitedly.

"Not yet," he heard Lily say. "He's holding up the floor."

"Holding up the floor?" he heard Audra say in confusion. A second later, her head popped around to peek in through the open pocket doors.

"Lifting the floor," he said with a chuckle as he stood. "I should know better than to use the terms I'd use with my brother at a job site." He stepped from the room. "How did it go?"

"We're making a pie!" Lily blurted out.

"You are?" Carter said, scooping her up in his arms. "And what kind of pie are you making?"

"One that wins," Mason told him.

He looked to Audra in confusion.

She laughed softly. "We're entering the town's annual pie bake-off."

He arched a brow. "You are?"

"You don't have to sound so surprised. I told you I could cook. And pies just happen to be one of my specialties," she said with a slight lift to her chin.

"I'm not surprised," he said honestly. "Just glad to see you're getting involved." Audra tended to keep to herself, content to spend most of her time at the house with her children. "It'll give you a chance to meet more people."

"I know," she said, nodding. "I've come to realize that I need to put more effort into fitting in, not only for my children, but for myself, as well."

"And it's for a good cause," he noted as he set Lily on her feet. "Why don't you kids go play while I fill your momma in on what I did on the house today?"

They didn't have to be told twice. The second they scampered off up the stairs, he motioned for Audra to follow him into the living room. "Watch your step."

Her eyes widened as she took in the entire room. "You did all this while we were away?"

"Amazing how a good, home-cooked breakfast and a pretty female can motivate a man to put some real work in."

Audra turned away, falling silent.

"Darlin'?"

"Please don't do that," she said softly, keeping her gaze averted.

"I'll try not to," he said, studying her with a frown. "But first you've gotta explain to me what it is I've done to upset you."

"Calling me *darlin',*" she said. "And saying… well, that I'm pretty."

His mouth quirked up into a grin once more. "*Darlin'* just happens to be common Texan speak," he explained. Yet, with her, it felt like more. "And my momma raised me to never tell a lie. You're pretty. That's a fact. I won't apologize for telling the truth."

A blush filled her cheeks. "I'll try to remember that." Then her gaze shot up to meet his. "The darlin' part. Not the pretty part."

Carter chuckled. "Make note of both, darlin', because you are."

A small smile tugged at her lips. "Thank you for the compliment."

"My pleasure," he replied. "Now about this here floor of yours…"

Chapter Seven

"Working hard I see."

Carter paused in his work to glance up, finding Audra smiling down at him from the living room entryway, something he found himself looking forward to each time he came to work on her house. Three weeks of her beautiful smile, one that rivaled the sunlight when it came to lighting up a room, wasn't near enough. "Work hard. Play hard," he replied with a grin.

"I'm glad."

"So are most of Cooper Construction's customers." Setting the measuring tape he held in his hand onto the floor beside him, he straightened and stood.

"I wasn't referring to the 'work hard' part," she amended. "I'm glad you take the time to play hard and enjoy life. A lot of men don't." A flicker of sadness moved across her face before she glanced away. "Looks like I'll be putting down all new flooring."

Carter worked his way across what was left of the old living room floor to stand before her. "Not all men are like your ex."

Her gaze lifted to meet his and her soft smile returned. "I'm finding that out." She held up the plastic carryout bag she held in her hand. "I thought you might be hungry."

He chuckled. "Darlin', I'm always hungry. My brothers tell me I should be the size of a barn with as much as I eat. But I've told you before I don't want you spending your hard-earned money on buying me lunch, or wasting your time making me lunches."

Every day for the past two weeks, Audra had either brought him carryout she picked up when she ran out to pick up her children from school, or left a note taped to the front door, telling him his lunch was in the fridge. From egg salad for sandwiches to homemade potato-bacon soup. The woman could cook. He never thought he'd be thinking it, but this was a woman who could have honestly given his momma a run for her money in the kitchen.

"Part of our deal was you work for only the cost of supplies, which I still am not comfortable with, and in exchange I cook for you. And since I didn't have time to make lunch for you before I left this morning, you get this." She held the bag out to him. "Hope you like a meatball sub with extra provolone."

"Darlin'," he said with an exaggerated groan as he reached for the bag, "you know what they say about the way to a man's heart."

She stiffened visibly and Carter wanted to yank the words he'd just spoken back into his mouth.

"I should get going," she said, pulling her van keys from the purse slung over her shoulder.

"Audra," he said apologetically, knowing she wasn't looking to be part any man's heart. She'd made that pretty clear. Friendship was as far as anything could ever go between them. But he found himself wanting more. He chose his next words carefully. "I know what you've gone through and understand your need to be guarded. But the truth is, I'd like to move beyond a working relationship where you're concerned."

"Carter," she said in a panicked whisper, "please don't."

"Friendship, Audra," he said determinedly. "That's all I'm asking for. Like you, I'm not looking for anything more right now," he added, hoping it would ease her worry. It wasn't a lie. He knew that there would be no right now with her. But tomorrow, or the day after…well, that was another story.

"But we're already friends."

"We are," he agreed. "But I'd like the opportunity to get to know you better outside of our working together on your house. Maybe go to dinner or a movie. With the kids, of course."

She looked surprised. "You'd include them?"

"Wouldn't have it any other way." Her children were her world. Their acceptance of him was every bit as important as Audra's. "Besides, I think we should be able to fit in some alone time on the front porch swing after we get back from our friends-only date. Time to talk without having to shout over my power tools."

"Isn't there some sort of policy at your company about not mixing business with…" She hesitated, as if searching for the right word.

"Friendship?" he responded with a grin. Though he understood her wariness. He felt the same sense of panic himself at the thought of taking a chance with his heart. But try as he might to ignore the feelings she stirred in him, they refused to go away. Maybe it was time to take a chance. Only with Audra, that meant starting from the ground up. "I own the company," he reminded her. "If there were such a policy against becoming friends with a client, I'd waste no time in changing it."

"Oh."

"Audra, my wanting to take our acquaintance to a deeper level shouldn't equate in your mind to having someone threaten to toss you into a den of hissing, writhing rattlesnakes."

His teasing had her features easing, a small smile pulling once more at her rosy lips. "That might be exaggerating things just a bit," she replied. "It feels more along the line of deep-sea diving without a tank."

"Ah, so much better," he teased and then grew serious once more. "So it's a good thing for you that our friendship is gonna take place on dry land. How about I give you and the kids a lift to church this Sunday and then to the pie bake-off later in the afternoon?"

"I have to come back home after church to bake my pie. Maybe we could meet you at the bake-off."

"I've got a better idea," he countered. "How about if I bring you home after Sunday services and do some work around the house while you and the kids do your baking?"

"You are not going to work on a Sunday," she said, sounding appalled by the very thought of it.

"Why not? You'll be working in the kitchen."

"That's not work," she replied. "I enjoy spending my free time cooking."

He leaned in closer, resting a forearm against the pocket-door frame beside her. "And I happen to enjoy spending my free time working on your house."

"Impossible man," she muttered as she looked up at him.

"Plucky female," he said with a teasing grin.

Her gaze locked on his, and then she blinked as if trying to collect her thoughts. A second later, she was backing away out into the entryway. "I have to run. School will be out in a few minutes."

He nodded, watching as she practically flew out the door. It was a good thing she'd run when she had, because the sudden urge to kiss her had nearly overrun his plan to take things slow. And nothing meant more to him than doing right by Audra and those two adorable kids of hers. That meant making certain he knew what it was he really wanted, because seeing them truly happy in their new life had moved to being first and foremost in his mind.

"Knock knock."

Audra glanced up from the note she'd been making for the reverend, who wouldn't be back to the church until after Audra had gone home for the day, to find Lizzie standing in the doorway of the church's office. She smiled in greeting. "This is a change. I'm usually coming to your place of work."

The young waitress, dressed in her Big Dog's uniform, apron and all, stepped into the room. "I've been meaning to swing by and get signed up for the annual pie-baking contest, but by the time my work shift ends I'm rushing home to do schoolwork. Since we're getting down to the wire and two o'clock is pretty much downtime at the restaurant, Mrs. Simms sent me over here to get us both signed up. Not that I'm much of a cook," she admitted. "But I really wanna see that new rec center get built. So I'll pay the fee and hope not to make the judges swear off pie for good after they've tasted mine."

Audra laughed softly. "Your cooking can't be that bad."

"It is," Lizzie said with a dramatic sigh. "Just ask Verna. That's why she keeps me out front waiting tables."

Verna Simms owned Big Dog's. A middle-aged widow with a passion for cooking, she spent most of her time back in the restaurant's kitchen whipping up her customers' orders.

"I have the forms right here," Audra said, pulling two from the stack of preprinted papers. "The kids and I are signed up for the competition, as well," she said with a smile as she handed them to Lizzie.

"How fun! I'll bet they're excited."

Audra nodded. "You have no idea."

"So how are things coming along at the new house?" Lizzie asked.

"If only it were a new house," Audra said, laughing softly. Thanks to Carter, she no longer felt overwhelmed by the work the old house required. His coming into her life had been such a godsend. For both her and her children. "But things are moving right along," she said, answering the other woman's question. "I don't think there's anything Carter can't do." Ballet and baseball included, she thought with a smile.

"Funny, but I seem to recall him saying the very same thing about you when he stopped by Big Dog's with his niece last weekend," Lizzie said with a sly grin.

"He did?"

She nodded. "Let me see," she said as if trying to recall his exact words, "you're raising two children on your own while holding down a full-time job, your cooking rivals his momma's, which, by the way, is one of the biggest compliments a man can give a woman, you have no problem with getting your hands dirty while working alongside him on your house renovations and you can throw a wicked curveball."

A wicked curveball. Audra fought the urge to snicker at that last compliment. Her so-called wicked curveball was the result of a poorly thrown baseball, nothing intentional on her part. "Carter Cooper has a tendency to bend reality to his way of thinking."

"I think he's sweet on you," Lizzie teased.

Audra shook her head. "He's just a good man with a never-ending supply of kind words."

Lizzie eyed her skeptically.

"He's been very up-front about his not looking for a relationship," she added, feeling the need to stop any rumors before they started. No matter how much she wished what Lizzie was saying was true, there was still a part of her afraid to put her trust completely in another man. "Neither am I," she added, more for herself than anything else.

"Sorry," the younger woman was quick to apologize. "Despite the lack of a love life to call my own, I'm still a romantic at heart."

"No need to apologize," Audra assured her with a confirming smile.

"I guess I'll see you Sunday." She started for the door, pausing to call back over her shoulder, "Carter has a thing for pecan pie. Just so you know." Then with a fluttery wave of her hand, she was gone.

Pecan pie? Her specialty. Too bad Carter wasn't going to be one of the judges who would be deciding on the winner of Braxton's annual pie bake-off. Maybe she'd bake two pies on Sunday. One for the competition and one for dinner that evening. He deserved a special treat for all the hard work he'd been doing on her house the past few weeks.

She couldn't help but feel guilty about the amount of time her home repairs had taken up in his life. Now that his and Nathan's company was contracted for another job, Carter had been coming by in the evenings and weekends to do what he could do.

In addition to some much-needed plumbing work, Carter had replaced almost all of the living room subfloor and then put down the wood-look laminate that Audra had chosen, one guaranteed to wear well with two young children running over it. He'd also made adjustments to the beautiful, old oak pocket doors so they now slid open and closed with very little effort, and caulked all the windows as a temporary fix until fall when she would invest in replacement windows before the cold months set in.

All in all, the inside repairs were coming along quite nicely, thanks to Carter's expertise and hard work. Outside was another matter. The roof still needed to be repaired in several places. But with the last bit of daylight ending shortly after eight in the evening, Carter had limited time to see to her roof by the time he got there after work and ate the dinner she usually had ready for him.

The phone rang, bringing Audra from her thoughts. "Church office. This is Audra speaking. How can I help you?" she answered as Mrs. Johns had instructed her to.

"You can help me by joining me and my family for dinner tonight."

"Carter?"

"Expecting a dinner invitation from someone else?"

She laughed at his teasing remark. "Hardly."

He chuckled. "How's work going?"

"Really well," she said. "It's worked out so wonderfully with the kids being able to come here after school."

"Happy for you," he said with all sincerity. "I don't wanna keep you since you're still at work, but I wanted to catch you before you left for home and started making dinner. Nathan asked me to bring you and the kids over to his place for dinner. A pizza party to be exact."

"That's so kind of him to include us."

"Nice of Katie," he explained. "Not that Nathan wasn't more than happy to invite you and the kids over, but this whole pizza party thing was Katie's idea. A sure way for her to get to play with her new friends. I'm sure you've picked up from the times Nathan and Katie stopped by that he'd do just about anything to make his baby girl happy."

"Ha!" she replied. "You're a fine one to talk, *Uncle* Carter. I'd say you and Logan give your big brother a pretty good run for his money when it comes to making Katie happy."

"Reckon we might at that," he admitted with a husky chuckle. "So can I tell Katie she'll have some playmates this evening?"

"I'm sure Lily and Mason would love spending time with Katie. And pizza sounds wonderful."

"I'm gonna take that as a yes," Carter replied. "I'll give Nathan a call and let him know. I know the kids have school tomorrow, so we won't be too late getting home. In fact, I hope to get those hinges on the bathroom towel cupboard before I head home tonight."

Getting home. Those words sounded so right. As if Carter was a part of her family. If only their lives before meeting each other had been different, maybe then… Audra shook the wistful thought from her head. It would never be their home. He wasn't looking for a family. Just a friend. She needed to keep that foremost in her mind.

"Five thirty good to pick you and the kids up?" Carter asked, drawing her from her thoughts.

"That should be fine. We'll see you then."

"See you then," he repeated and then ended the call.

Audra had just settled back against the padded chair behind the small metal desk when her son appeared in the doorway. "Is it time to go home yet?"

Her gaze shifted to the clock and then back to her son. "Almost. By the time you and Lily get all the toys you've been playing with picked up and put away in the playroom, it'll be time to leave."

"Do you think Mr. Cooper will be there when we get home?"

She smiled, understanding her son's eagerness to see Carter. She looked forward to seeing him in the evenings, as well. Dinner conversations were even more enjoyable with another adult there to share her day with. "Not right when we get home, but he's going to be picking us up to go to a pizza party."

"A pizza party!" her son exclaimed.

Audra's smile widened as she added, "At Katie's."

Mason whooped with delight.

"Shh…" she said, quickly shushing him. "Remember where you are. Now go help Lily clean up while I finish the last of my work for the day."

He didn't have to be told twice, disappearing from the doorway as quietly as he'd appeared. Audra knew the feeling. She, too, was looking forward to spending time with Carter Cooper and his gentle smile and warm heart. Even if all they could ever be was friends.

"Katie!" Lily exclaimed as Carter lowered her from the backseat of the extended cab truck. The second her feet touched the ground, she was off and running toward Nathan's house, where Katie stood waving wildly from the front porch.

Mason didn't wait to be helped down. Throwing open the back passenger door on his side, he practically leaped from the truck in his eagerness to catch up with his sister.

"You think they're a little excited to be here?" he said with a grin as he opened Audra's door for her.

"Beyond," she replied with a smile. "They love spending time with Katie. They're like three peas in a pod. I'm so glad your brother's been able to bring her by to see them on occasion. I've enjoyed visiting with him while the kids played."

An unexpected surge of something feeling uncomfortably close to jealousy rushed through him. While he'd been growing fonder and fonder of Audra and her two adorable children, had he overlooked something he should have considered? There was no denying how much Nathan and Audra had in common. Both were single parents raising young children. Both would do almost anything to see their children happy. Children who had bonded with each other almost immediately upon meeting.

Carter didn't like the direction his thoughts were taking, but he also loved his brothers enough to put his own feelings aside if it meant guaranteeing theirs. If Nathan was finally at the point where he was ready to move on with his life and start over with someone new, would he consider doing so with Audra?

The possibility didn't sit well in Carter's gut, but he had given his word to Isabel to look after Nathan and Katie. If Audra could make his big brother happy again, then his wants and needs didn't matter. Especially when he was still trying to figure out exactly what his own wants and needs were when it came to Audra. His brother deserved to be happy. As did she. What kind of man would he be if he stood in the way of their possible happiness?

"Carter?" Audra said, searching his face.

Snapping out of his thoughts, he dropped his gaze to her pretty face. And he knew at that moment that being a selfless man when it came to her was going to take every bit of grit he had in him.

"Is something wrong?" she asked.

He looked down into those beautiful amber-flecked eyes and felt a sharp tug at his heart. Was something wrong? Only the fact that he was about to push her, a woman he'd grown overly fond of during their time spent together, in his brother's direction.

"Uncle Carter!" Katie called out through the screen door. "Hurry up! The pizza's gonna get cold!"

Grateful for the interruption, he turned from Audra and forced a smile. "On our way!"

They started for the house in silence.

Carter felt Audra's gaze straying in his direction several times, but kept his own focused on getting inside.

The screen door swung open as they stepped up onto the porch. Nathan stood there smiling. "Glad you and the kids could make it," he said to Audra in a warm greeting.

"I'm so glad you invited us," she replied with a polite smile.

Her words elicited another tug at Carter's heart. Let it go, he told himself. You're doing the right thing. And if he told himself that often enough, then maybe, just maybe, he would be able to accept it without feeling as though a herd of bulls was stampeding through his gut.

His brother stepped aside, motioning them into the house. "The kids are already in the dining room with paper plates at the ready."

Audra laughed. "And if we wait much longer to join them, I'm not promising there will be any pizza left."

"I'm sure Millie has things under control," Nathan replied.

"Millie's here?" Audra inquired as they stepped inside.

He nodded. "She's been looking forward to spending some time getting to know you outside of Sunday service hellos."

Millie was like family to the Coopers and had become a substitute grandmother for Katie, watching her when Katie was off from school and Nathan had to work. A close neighbor of his parents for as long as Carter could remember, Millie's husband had been the only other fatality that day the tornado struck Braxton.

They made their way through the living room and into the dining area, where the children sat hungrily eyeing up the open boxes of pizza. Seven places had been set from paper plates to napkins to glasses of freshly brewed sweet tea.

Millie glanced up with a warm smile. "Hello, dear. So glad to see you."

"Same here," Audra replied.

Playing host, Nathan pulled out the chair next to Millie's and motioned for Audra to sit down. "Have a seat."

"Thank you," she said as she settled onto it.

Carter watched, noting how at ease his brother was with Audra. And her with him. Then his gaze moved to the lone empty seat beside hers. Instead of taking it as he might have before realization settled on him like a falling boulder, Carter made his way around to the vacant chair on the opposite side of the table, leaving Nathan no choice but to settle himself onto the empty chair next to Audra's.

Carter met Audra's questioning gaze from across the table and shifted uncomfortably, clearing his throat. "Pizza sure smells good."

"Can we eat now?" Lily asked, her tiny hands gripping the sides of the paper plate in front of her.

"Not until we've said a quick prayer of thanks," Audra responded, tipping her head downward.

This time it was Nathan who was shifting uneasily in his seat, meeting Carter's knowing gaze. His brother had given up on prayer after losing Isabel. In fact, the only reason he attended church every Sunday was for the sake of his young daughter, who Isabel had wanted to be raised with faith in the Lord. It was something Nathan no longer clung to himself.

Katie, oblivious to her father's discomfort, bowed her tiny head in prayer as did Mason and Lily.

Carter offered up a sympathetic smile before joining the others in prayer.

"Nathan," Audra said, "would you like to offer up our thanks?"

"I'll do it," Carter offered and then, without another moment's hesitation, set to thanking the Lord for the blessings He had bestowed upon them.

Amens rippled around the table as the prayer ended.

His brother's determination to turn his back on the Lord might be an issue for Audra. Carter hoped that if things should move in that direction the love of another good Christian woman would bring his brother around.

Audra's love. Carter found himself envying his brother for something that hadn't even happened yet. Might never happen.

"Now can we eat?" Lily asked eagerly.

Carter chuckled, grateful for the reprieve from the direction his thoughts had taken. "*Now* we can eat."

They filled their plates with slices of still-warm pepperoni pizza and tossed salad.

"Mmm…" Audra groaned as she swallowed the bite of pizza she'd just taken. "And here I thought Chicago had the best pizza."

"The secret is in the crust," Millie told her.

"At least, that's what Ryan claims," Nathan muttered between bites.

"Ryan?" she replied as she reached for the glass of sweet tea in front of her.

"Logan's friend," Carter explained. "They went to school together."

Nathan nodded. "Thicker than thieves. At least, they used to be before becoming business owners. Less playtime for them these days."

"Ryan owns the local bowling alley/pizzeria—Ryan's Pies and Pins," Millie explained as she placed a second piece of pizza onto Katie's now-empty plate.

Audra smiled. "Bowling and pizza. Sounds like a perfect combination."

"I like to bowl," Mason announced between chews.

"Me, too," Katie chimed in.

"I don't know how." Lily sighed.

"You guys will have to take the kids bowling some time," Carter muttered, trying hard not to include himself in that mix.

"You don't bowl?" Audra asked, the barest hint of disappointment in her voice.

He shook his head, not meeting her gaze. "Not often. Nathan's a much better bowler than I am."

"Can we, Daddy?" Katie asked, looking up at her daddy with wide, pleading eyes.

Nathan glanced his way with a tempered frown. "I think Uncle Carter should be the one to take the lot of you bowling sometime, seeing as how he needs work on his bowling skills."

All eyes, Audra's included, swung in his direction. Three pairs of them expectant. One pair narrowed in irritation. That last pair, amber eyes surrounded by thick lashes, was filled with confusion as they watched him from across the table.

"Better they learn from the best," Carter replied, meeting Nathan's gaze. "And Nathan taught Katie how to bowl. I'm sure he'd be willing to teach Lily how to, as well."

Lily, who sat next to Carter, clapped her hands. "Yay!"

"You kids best eat your pizza before it gets cold," Nathan said. Then he pushed away from the table and stood. "Carter, I'd like to have a word with you outside."

"Sure thing." He set the piece of pizza he'd been working on down onto his plate and then rose to his feet. "We won't be long," he told their guests. "Got a few business matters to discuss. Best not done at the table."

Nathan followed him out onto the front porch, closing the door firmly behind them. "The only business we have to discuss is you needing to stay outta mine!" his brother growled. "What do you think you're doing?"

"You deserve to find happiness again," Carter replied.

"And you've decided I'll find it with Audra?"

"Katie adores Mason and Lily. You're both raising children alone," he explained. "Audra's sweeter than a ripe berry. And unerringly kind. She's determined and resilient, like the hardiest of wildflowers. And she's prettier than sunset over a lake."

Nathan studied him in silence.

"She's got a huge heart," he continued. "A sense of humor. And her smile..." he said, shaking his head. "Well, it's capable of making a man's knees weak."

His brother crossed his arms. "What I'm wondering is why you've got your mind set on stirring my interest in a woman you've clearly fallen for?"

"What?"

"You heard me. Can you honestly tell me Audra hasn't managed to snag a piece of your heart? Because only a man that finds himself falling for a woman would describe her with such flowery conviction."

"Flowery conviction?" He'd merely reminded Nathan of Audra's good qualities.

"Sweeter than ripe berries," his brother repeated. "Prettier than sunset over a lake. Fluff only a man whose heart has taken a leap would be spouting."

"She's a better fit for you," Carter argued with a frown. "You both have kids."

"I'm not looking for a relationship," Nathan said firmly, his dark brows creased into a frown. "I loved Isabel. I don't want another woman."

"But Katie—"

"Has me," his brother interrupted. "And you and Logan and Millie. Look," he said with a troubled sigh, "Audra's a wonderful woman who deserves to find true happiness, something it sounds like she never truly had in her marriage. But it won't be with me. And if you don't stop being such an idiot, it won't be with you, either." Nathan turned and went back inside, leaving Carter standing there alone.

"You were awfully quiet on the way home," Carter said as he walked Audra from his truck to her front porch, the children racing ahead of them.

"I didn't have anything to say," she replied stiffly.

"Audra?" he said worriedly.

She fell silent while she stepped past her children to unlock the door. But the second they raced inside to get ready for bed, she turned, blocking his way. "It's late. You should be heading home."

"There were a few things I planned to do around the house before I called it a night."

"I'm tired," she told him. "So I'm calling it a night for the both of us."

His gaze moved over her face, his concern deepening when he saw the hurt in her eyes. "What's wrong?"

"We're both adults," she told him. "If I somehow made you feel uncomfortable, made you think I wanted more from you than friendship, then I apologize. It wasn't intentional. You've made it very clear where you stand on the matter. But instead of talking to me about whatever it is I've done, you try to push me in your brother's direction in a manner so blatantly obvious…" She turned away with a sniffle. "Go home, Carter."

"Audra," he said, placing his hands on her shoulders as he stepped up behind her, "I never meant to hurt you. I only meant…" He let his words trail off. How was he supposed to explain his reasons for doing what he'd done?

"To send me a message," she answered for him. "Well, message received loud and clear."

He turned her to face him, heart wrenching at the sight of tears shimmering in her beautiful eyes. "I promised Isabel."

She blinked. "What?"

"I promised to keep her family safe and happy." Releasing her, Carter walked over to the porch railing, looking out into the darkness that now blanketed the town. "I was the one to find Isabel that day. The sky was still dark and rain was coming down in sheets, making it hard to see. I almost missed seeing her there, lying under the scattered debris that had once been my parents' home." Reaching out, he curled his hands atop the weathered railing, gripping it tightly as he replayed that moment in his mind. "She was still alive…barely."

"Carter," Audra said behind him, his name a mere whisper in the night.

"She was so broken," he continued, choking up as he spoke the words he'd kept to himself since that horrible day. "The festive Christmas sweater she had worn that day to help my parents decorate for the holidays was covered in mud and blood and splintered shards of wood."

He squeezed his eyes shut, trying to block out the image that had burned itself into his mind.

Slender arms moved about his waist as Audra stepped forward to offer her comforting embrace. She laid her head against his back, saying softly, "I'm so sorry you had to be the one to find her that day."

"Better me than my brother," he rasped out, the words filled with emotion. Just having her there gave him the courage to lay his long-held-in pain out on the table. "It would have killed Nathan to see her like that. Killed him to watch her struggle to breathe, her face pinched tight with pain before slipping away. So I kept the truth to myself, letting him believe she had passed away before I had gotten to her."

"Oh, Carter," she said sadly. Her arms tightened around him in a compassionate hug. "In my heart, I believe the good Lord put you there for a reason. Not only to protect your brother from more emotional pain, but to offer comfort to Isabel. If only in your promise to look after Nathan and Katie. A promise I have faith gave her a much-needed sense of peace in her final moments."

With a heavy sigh, he turned and cupped her upturned face. "You are a very special woman, Audra Marshall."

"And you're a very special man, Carter Cooper," she said, her words soft and soothing.

"My brother's a good man, too" he said.

Her arms fell away as Audra took a step back. "Your brother is a good man, but he's not the man for me. Love can't be forced, Carter," she said sadly. "I know that better than anyone."

"Audra…" he began, wishing he could take back the words. Take back his halfhearted attempts to direct her interest in his brother's direction.

"Please," she said, "hear me out. When your brother is ready to love again, *if* he's ever ready to love again, he'll find the happiness Isabel wanted for him. You can't push him before he's ready and you can't choose for him. All you can do is support and love him."

She was right. Deep down, he knew that. And despite all his good intentions, Carter couldn't help but feel relieved that Audra didn't see Nathan as the man for her. *Could she see him as that man?* he wondered. Did he want to be that man?

"And since I value honesty," she went on, "I'm going to take this conversation one step further. I think you should consider telling Nathan the truth." Before he could utter a word of argument against doing so, she continued, "I think he would find comfort in knowing Isabel didn't die alone and afraid. Because in your brother's mind, that's how her life ended. Let him know she had someone there to hold her hand as the Lord welcomed her home."

"I'd never thought about it that way," he admitted hoarsely. Then, with a nod, he said, "I'll consider it."

"I'll pray for you to find the strength to do so," she said softly. "Thank you again for including us at your family dinner tonight." That said, Audra let herself inside and then turned to peer out at him through the screen door. "Good night, Carter." Then she disappeared from view as the heavy wooden door closed between them.

Chapter Eight

Carter felt like a teen again, preparing for his very first date. Only this date had far more importance. It was a step, a very determined step, toward his future happiness.

He glanced toward the gathering of women on the sidewalk outside of the church. Audra stood among them, happily chattering away. It was good to see her settling in and making friends. Good to see her happy. Even if she hadn't been near as happy with him since his attempt to match her up with his brother several days before. Not that she had said anything to make him feel that way. It was the way she busied herself with other tasks whenever he was there working on the house in the evenings, instead of offering to help the way she used to. Not that he needed help. What he needed was *her*. Her smile. Her company. Just her.

Today he would be telling her just that.

"Just can't take your eyes off her, can you?"

He turned to find Logan standing there, a wide grin splitting his tanned face. "Appears that way," he replied with an equally wide grin.

His younger brother's eyes widened. "You're admitting it?"

"Yep." He slid his gaze back toward the gaggle of females.

"Well, I'll be," Logan muttered. "So you two an item now?"

"No," he replied, not taking his eyes off Audra. "But by the end of today we will be."

His brother sidled up closer. "You're serious?"

"As a heart attack."

"What happened to steering clear of anything serious? Didn't you learn anything from what happened to Nathan?"

Dragging his gaze away from Audra, he sighed. He understood his brother's confusion. During those dark days following their parents' and Isabel's deaths, he and his brothers had made a pact to avoid letting any females close to their hearts. No risk. No loss. But something had changed. At least, for him it had.

"I learned that there are no guarantees in life and that if you're blessed enough to find the kind of happiness Nathan had with Isabel you should grab on to it with both hands."

He didn't think it possible, but his brother's eyes widened even more. "You're in love with Audra?"

"I didn't say that," he said, looking around to make certain no one was within hearing distance of their conversation. "Not yet anyways. I intend to take this thing one step at a time. At the moment, Audra and I are friends. Today, after the pie judging contest, if everything goes as I hope it will, we're gonna be more than friends."

"I have to admit I'm not surprised," Logan replied with a sigh, his gaze following Carter's across the churchyard. "She's a good woman. Reckon she'll lead you down the right road," he added with a grin.

"The road to happiness," Carter muttered in agreement.

As if sensing she was being watched, Audra glanced their way and smiled.

"She's right pretty, too," Logan added.

"No argument here."

"And fortunate," his brother said, his grin widening. "Not many females find themselves a man who's willing to do pirouettes for them. Or should I say, for their little girl?"

That had Carter's head snapping around.

"Audra told you about that?" Not that he regretted allowing Lily to choose the type of dancing they would be doing. She'd been in her glory and they'd all laughed so hard that day.

"Lily did," his brother said. "That little girl thinks the sun rises and sets with you."

That warmed his heart. "I happen to think she's pretty special, too."

"Speaking of special," his brother said with a chuckle, "Lily and her two squealing little sidekicks are heading this way."

Carter turned, opening his arms as Lily and Katie launched themselves at him in a flurry of frilly Sunday dresses. Mason stopped beside Logan, folding his tiny arms across his chest the way his brother had his. The cowboy hat Audra had purchased for her son the day before, one that very closely resembled Logan's, was pulled low on the little boy's brow.

"Appears I'm not the only one the sun rises and sets with," Carter said with a chuckle.

Logan, who had at one time dreamed of having a slew of his own children running around, grinned down at Mason. "Nice hat, cowboy."

Mason beamed at the compliment.

"We're ready to go bake our pie," Lily announced, looking up at him.

"Let's go see if your momma's ready to go."

"Can I go, too?" Katie said longingly. "I wanna help bake a pie."

"Can she, please?" Lily whined.

"Reckon that's something you'd best ask your momma," Carter replied as he started for the slowly disbanding group of females in front of the church, the two precious bundles of lace and brightly colored fluff held securely in his arms.

"She'll say yes if you ask," Mason told him as he and Logan walked alongside him.

That's what he was hoping for. But it had nothing to do with making pies and everything to do with making a new path in the life he'd thought he had all planned out.

"Sure smells good."

Audra glanced toward the open doorway to see Carter poking his head into the kitchen. "Aren't you supposed to be working?" she asked as she placed the oversize cookie sheet that held the pies they'd just baked atop the stove.

"I was," he replied, stepping farther into the room. "But a man can only take so much before the smell of hot-in-the-oven pecan pie lures him away from the task at hand. Even if he's not able to do any more than take in its mouth-watering scent."

"Must be your day," she told him. "It just so happens we made two of them."

"One for the contest and one for dessert tonight," Mason explained from where he and the girls sat taking turns rolling out the leftover pie dough just for fun.

"That so," Carter muttered, his gaze meeting hers. "Appears I'm gonna have to finagle myself a dinner invitation."

"No finagling needed," Audra replied. "You're welcome to join us." He wouldn't be sharing dinners with them much longer as work on her house, at least on the inside, was almost done. Maybe he could still come around, seeing as how they were friends, and join them for an occasional meal.

"Tell you what," he said, snapping her out of her contemplative thoughts. "You've spent half the afternoon in this kitchen, toiling over a hot stove. How about I pick up some fried chicken and a few sides and bring them out with me this evening?"

"I can't ask you to bring dinner for all of us," she replied. "Katie's going to be joining us, as well."

"What's one more leg of chicken?" he countered with that slightly crooked grin that never failed to make her knees weak. "Katydid doesn't eat much. Do you, Katydid?" he asked, looking her way.

His niece shook her head in agreement. "But I'd like some pie."

"There you go," he told Audra. "I'll pick up dinner later this evening, after you've all had time to recover from the bake-off. You've already got dessert covered so I'd say we're all set."

She was feeling spent from her rush to get the pies made in time for that afternoon's bake-off. Not having to cook dinner later that evening would be a welcome respite. "All right, Carter. Dinner's on you tonight. Thank you."

"Anytime." He stepped closer to the stove, closer to her, and then leaned past her, sniffing the air. "Correct me if I'm wrong, but do I detect a little something extra in this pecan pie? Jelly beans, perhaps?" he proposed with a playful grin as his gaze shifted back to the children.

"Uncle Carter," Katie said with an eye roll. "You don't put jelly beans in a pie."

"You've never tried one of my pies. My specialty is broccoli-and-blueberry pie," he said with a wink in Audra's direction.

"Eeew!" the children exclaimed in near unison, their little faces scrunching up in disgust.

Audra laughed. "Our pie isn't nearly as creative. Maybe you should have considered entering the bake-off."

He chuckled. "There's always next year."

"And since you aren't judging, I think we'd be safe in telling you we're going to be entering my salted caramel toasted pecan pie."

He placed a hand to his chest with a deep groan. "Ah, a sure way to any man's heart."

"Unless that man isn't looking for more than friendship," Audra muttered as she turned to the sink. Oh, why had she said that? Reaching out, she turned on the sink and reached for the dish soap.

Carter beat her to it, handing over the plastic squeeze bottle with a warm smile. "It just so happens that this man is." Letting go, he strode from the kitchen.

Heart racing, Audra watched him go. He wanted more? The thought both frightened and excited her. In her visions of the future, she had never once conjured up another man in her life. Her dreams consisted mostly of a new life in Texas for her children. Her own happiness had never really been a consideration. Maybe because she had spent so many years accepting her lot in life instead dreaming of what could be.

Audra finished cleaning up the kitchen, then hurried upstairs with the children to get cleaned up. Carter had gone outside to do a walk-around inspection of the house's exterior to see what needed to be done before they headed back into town. She found herself glancing out the upstairs windows in search of him as she stood brushing her hair, his words still clinging to her thoughts—*it just so happens that this man is*.

Was she? Did she really want to move what they had beyond the close friendship they'd formed and risk losing a man she had come to care a great deal for? Closing her eyes, she said a silent prayer for the Lord to help guide her down the right path.

"We're ready!"

Audra turned from the window to find Lily, Mason and Katie standing in the open doorway to her bedroom. "Then we'd best get going," she said as she returned the hairbrush to the mirrored vanity tray atop her dresser.

With excited squeals, they spun around and raced down the steps. They were already out the front door before she was even halfway down the stairs. She headed into the kitchen to grab the basket she'd tucked the still-warm pie into.

Carter met her on the porch, taking the square wicker basket from her as he walked her out to the truck. "I'll put this in the back," he said as he opened the front passenger door for her. "The kids are already belted in."

With a smile, she climbed up onto the bench seat and buckled herself in, as well. She was looking forward to this afternoon, spending it with her new friends and hopefully making new acquaintances. Even if they didn't win the bake-off. She just hoped the children wouldn't be too disappointed if their pie wasn't chosen for the blue ribbon.

When they arrived at the park on the outskirts of town, where the festivities were being held, Audra's mouth dropped open. One large, open-sided tent and several smaller ones dotted the tree-shaded grass. The larger one was most likely for the pie judging. The smaller ones were a mix of food stands and items being offered for sale. And one other tent was filled with an assortment of picnic baskets with colorful bows tied around their handles. Raffle items perhaps?

"Looks like a good turnout," Carter noted as he helped her down from the truck.

"I didn't expect all of this," she mumbled in amazement as she took in the scene in front of them. The quiet little tree-filled park was filled with people milling about. It appeared the entire town had chosen to attend that afternoon's festivities.

Carter smiled as he moved to let the children out. "The folks of Braxton are pretty good about supporting a good cause." Turning, he lifted Lily out and set her on the ground, doing the same with Mason and Katie.

"Wow!" Mason gasped, eyes wide.

"It's a fair!" Lily exclaimed.

"It's a bake-off," Katie amended. "Fairs have Ferris wheels."

"Not all fairs," Carter told her.

"Just the fun fairs," Mason muttered as he looked around.

"There's a petting zoo," Carter said, pointing to a small area that had been set up with a temporary fence to contain a large woolly sheep and several adorable little pygmy goats.

That seemed to stir her son's interest. Lily's and Katie's, as well.

"What do you say we go check out the petting zoo and then take a walk down to the duck pond while your momma heads over to the judging tent to get signed in?" Carter asked, sending a warm smile Audra's way.

"Ducks!" Lily exclaimed.

"Don't go too close to the water," Audra warned and then lifted her gaze back to his. "She can't swim."

"Reckon we'll just have to teach her how

once the weather warms up a little more. Water's still a might cold yet this time of year."

"Teach me, too," Mason insisted.

"I can teach you," Katie said, puffing up her little chest. "I've been swimming since I was a baby."

Carter chuckled. "Tell you what, Katydid, how about you and I teach them how to swim together when the time comes? That is, if it's all right with their momma."

Audra hesitated, torn between knowing that her children should know how to swim and her fear of how quickly water could take away those you love.

"Can they, Mommy?" Lily asked.

"We'll see" was all she could commit to at that moment.

"Why don't you kids head on over to the petting zoo?" Carter suggested, not taking his gaze from her. "I'll join you in a moment."

With enthusiastic nods, the children made a squealing beeline toward the animals' temporary pen.

"I'm a good swimmer," Carter said when they were out of hearing range. "And you already know I've had first-aid training."

"It's not you," she said with a sigh. "It's me. My parents drowned in Lake Michigan the summer after I graduated from high school."

His smile faded as he reached for her hand. "I'm so sorry."

"It's okay. It's just that I haven't been in the water, not even in a pool, since that day. That's why my children don't know how to swim."

Frowning, he said, "I would never have suggested teaching them how to swim if I had known. I truly am sorry."

She gave his hand a gentle squeeze. "Don't be. They should know how to swim. Especially with us having that pond at the back of the property. One I've warned them never to go near. So, if the offer still stands, I'd like for you to be the one to teach them. I trust you to keep my children safe."

"That means a lot," he said, his voice rough with emotion.

"Audra!"

They turned to see Lizzie and an older woman, who Audra was certain she remembered seeing occasionally at Sunday services, walking toward them. Lizzie held a cardboard pie box in her hands, her entry for the bake-off, no doubt.

Releasing her hold on Carter's hand, she greeted her new friend with a smile. "Hello."

"Lizzie," Carter greeted with a nod.

"Hey, Carter," she greeted and then turned her attention back to Audra. "So glad I caught you before you went into the judging tent. I wanted to introduce the two of you. Momma, this is Audra Marshall. Audra, my momma, Mrs. Parker."

Her mother? Audra would never have guessed that. Her mother looked to be in her mid-to-late sixties. Grandmother maybe. Lizzie must have been one of those late-in-life babies.

"Rosalee," Lizzie's mother insisted with a warm smile. "I've seen you at church, but I always have to rush out afterward to get home to my husband."

"Daddy had a stroke a while back and doesn't get around as well as he used to," Lizzie explained.

"I'm sorry to hear that," Audra replied, her heart going out to them.

"The good Lord never gives us more than we can handle," Lizzie's mother said with a glance toward Carter. "James and I simply had to learn to live our lives a little differently than we had been. Anyway, it's so nice to finally have the chance to meet you."

"Same here," Audra said with a smile. Lizzie's mom was every bit as outgoing and friendly as her daughter. But they looked nothing alike. Rosalee looked Hispanic, while Lizzie had fair skin and light blue eyes with a light sprinkling of freckles across her smiling face. And her friend was tall and slender, whereas her mother couldn't be much over five feet and was more full-figured than her daughter.

Rosalee Parker's dark eyes shifted, coming to rest on the handsome cowboy beside Audra. "Afternoon, Carter."

"Ma'am," he said with a polite tip of his cowboy hat. "Looking as pretty as ever, I see."

"Oh, you smooth-talking Cooper boys," the older woman said, clicking her tongue, yet her smile widened at the compliment. "The single women in this town don't stand a chance." Looking to Audra, she said with a teasing grin, "You'd best watch yourself around this young man or you'll find yourself swept right off your feet."

Too late, she thought. She'd already been swept.

Lizzie's gaze settled on the basket hanging from Audra's hand and then she looked up at Audra. "You haven't checked in yet?"

Audra shook her head. "Not yet. We just got here."

"Great. We can check in together."

"While you girls do that," her mother said, "I'm off to the quilt raffle booth the ladies' quilting club set up. I volunteered to sell raffle tickets during the bake-off and auction. Hope to hear one of you girls took home the blue ribbon today." With a wave, she walked away.

"I'm headed over to watch the kids play with some pint-size goats," Carter told them. "We'll be over when the judging begins." Turning, he headed toward the petting zoo, where her children and Katie were kneeling by the fence to pet a little attention-seeking pygmy goat.

Audra watched him go, biting at her bottom lip.

"He's really good with kids," Lizzie said as she moved to stand beside her.

"I know. And my kids adore him," she said with a sigh.

Lizzie laughed. "You say that like it's a bad thing."

"It is if they're hoping for more." She turned to Lizzie. "Carter and I are friends. Good friends, but neither of us is looking for anything long-term."

"So you'd refuse him if he had a change of heart and wanted more?"

When Audra hesitated in answering, Lizzie grinned. "I didn't think so. Now come on. Let's go check in. I need extra time to schmooze the judges. My pie crust browned a little too much while I was distracted by a class project I was working on."

That had the smile returning to Audra's face as she walked with her friend to the judging tent.

"Hello, ladies," the reverend greeted when they stepped into the oversize tent.

"Reverend," they replied.

"Your spots are across from Mrs. Simms," he said, pointing them in the direction of the far side of the open-sided tent. The covered space had been lined with a long row of folding tables on each side for contestants to place their entries on. A handful of men and women, no doubt judges for that day's competition, stood milling about with clipboards clutched to their chests as arriving entrants found their assigned space and began setting their pies out for display and tasting.

Audra recognized several of the women from church as they moved through the tent. She said her hellos and was introduced by Lizzie to the women she didn't know. Edna Clark, whose husband owned The Toy Box, the local toy store, and was on Braxton's town council. Lacy Miller, a woman who looked to be in her midthirties and worked for Doctor Timmons as his receptionist and billing clerk. The Cooper boys' beloved Millie, with her kind smile. And Verna Simms, who had been assigned a spot directly across the tent from hers and Lizzie's.

One by one, the other entrants arrived. Soon, pies lined the tables. Ones with fancy lattice crusts on top, some with fluffy meringue, others with sugary sweet fruit toppings.

A younger woman rushed into the tent in a near panic, drawing Audra's gaze that direction. Reverend Johns walked over to greet her, pointing her to an open spot not far from where the judging table sat.

"That's Autumn Myers," Lizzie whispered as they lifted their pies from the protective nests they'd been stored in. "One half of Braxton's only set of identical twins. They went to high school with Logan."

"She's very pretty."

"They both are," Lizzie agreed. "At least Summer was the last time I saw her. But they are identical twins, so you have to figure she'd still resemble her twin. Summer lit out of town several years ago, but no one ever said why."

"That must be hard for her sister. Especially with them being twins and all."

Lizzie nodded. "Never more evident than when Autumn started her own realty company here in town, one I guess they had both talked about doing someday. She called it Twin Season Realty."

"I wish I would have gone through her rather than buy a house through an online auction."

"Then you never would have had Carter come to your rescue," her friend said with a grin.

"True." The memory of that day had Audra smiling. Carter's being a part of her life, of her children's lives, had been such a blessing. One she thanked the Lord for every day.

A few more contestants arrived, filling up the remainder of the vacant spaces at the tables. Lizzie made a conscious effort to tell her a little about each and every entrant.

There were so many faces and names, but Audra was determined to remember them all. Everyone had been so kind and welcoming to her since moving to Braxton. If there had ever been any doubt in her choice to move to Braxton, like the first moment she'd laid eyes on the auction home she'd purchased, she had none now. She felt like she belonged.

Mrs. Simms walked over to join them. "Your pie looks delicious," she said, eyeing Audra's entry.

"Thank you." She glanced around. "They all look delicious."

"Don't look at mine," Lizzie said with a smile.

Mrs. Simms shushed her. "Your pie looks just fine, Lizzie."

"If you like a firmer, darker crust," she countered. "No question as to why I wait on tables at your place instead of preparing the dishes."

"You're the best waitress in these parts," the older woman replied. "I don't know what I would have done without you all these years. I dread the thought of losing you to some news station after you graduate."

"At the rate I'm going, that day is still a long ways off," Lizzie said with a sigh.

"Your attention please," a thick-waisted woman in a parrot-green pantsuit announced in the microphone. "Everyone to your places. The judging is about to begin."

"That's Mrs. Danner," Mrs. Simms whispered. "She's a librarian at Braxton's public library. She's also this year's head judge."

Audra nodded, recalling her conversation with the reverend's wife. "Rachel mentioned that."

"Well, I'd best get back to my spot," the older woman said. "May the best pie win," she said with a smile before scurrying off.

"The judges will be making a walk-through to score the presentation of the entries," Mrs. Danner continued, her voice ringing out from the two overhead speakers at the front of the tent. "Once they have done so with your pie, please cut five small slices and place them on the five dessert plates stacked up in front of you. The judges will be back by to sample and score your pies. Lastly, we'd like to thank you all for contributing to this year's fund-raiser."

Audra couldn't contain her smile as she reached for the knife that had been placed next to the dessert plates and five plastic forks. "This is surprisingly nerve-wracking and fun all at the same time," she told Lizzie as she cut into her salted caramel toasted pecan pie.

People began to gather at the openings at the sides of the tent, watching as the judges made their way along the contestants' tables, tasting their awaiting slices of pie.

Just as the judges moved to sample her entry, Audra caught sight of Carter and the kids standing among the gathering crowd, his brothers flanking them. Carter bent to lift up Lily, holding her in the crook of his arm so she could see past Mason and Katie, who were jumping up and down in front of him in barely contained excitement. His warm smile widened.

Audra returned the smile and then forced her attention back to the half circle of judges in front of her. Returning their forks to their plates and the plates to the table, they made notes on their clipboards and then moved on to Lizzie's entry.

There had been no change in their expression

as they'd sampled her pie to know whether or not they liked her pie. Not even one little moan of delight. If they hadn't done the same thing with the other entrants' pies, Audra might have concluded they found her pie lacking.

Once the judging was complete, the five judges returned to their table at the front of the tent to tally up the contestants' scores. A few minutes later, Mrs. Danner stood, portable microphone in hand. "First, let me start by saying this wasn't an easy decision. The entries this year were all quite impressive. However, we had to narrow the field down and give recognition to the best of the best. So, without further ado, third place goes to Autumn Myers for her double-berry pie entry."

The crowd broke into applause as Reverend Johns stepped forward to place a white 3rd Place ribbon in front of her pie.

"Second place," Mrs. Danner said, "goes to a newcomer to our little town, Audra Marshall…" More clapping erupted.

Just past Mrs. Danner, the children's tiny shoulders sagged in disappointment.

"I would be remiss if I didn't make mention of Ms. Marshall's baking assistants," the older woman continued with a smile as she read from the bright pink notecard she held in her hands. "Congratulations to Mason and Lily Marshall and Katie Cooper." Her gaze sought them out in the crowd. "You talented little chefs can bake me a pie anytime."

That last comment seemed to take the sting out of their not winning. The soft pouts that had moved over the children's faces when learning their pie wouldn't be taking home the blue ribbon had been immediately replaced with beaming grins.

Reverend Johns came forward to lay the bright red 2nd Place ribbon in front of Audra, and mouthed, Congrats, before walking away.

"And the winner of this year's fund-raising competition—Braxton's twelfth annual pie bake-off—with her award winning apple-rhubarb crumb pie is Ms. Verna Simms."

Lizzie gave a little squeal of happiness for her boss.

Mrs. Simms was presented a crisp blue ribbon for her win, which she immediately hugged to her chest, her face filled with emotion.

Not winning had never felt so good, Audra thought with a smile. The joy on the older woman's face warmed her heart immensely.

"Thank you once again to all our entrants for supporting our cause. Now if you will please box up the remainder of your pies in the bakery boxes that Mr. Halverstadt will be handing out, we will move on to the next part of our fund-raising campaign—the pie auction. This year's auction will be slightly different thanks to the generosity of Cooper Construction. Prefilled lunch baskets and picnic blankets have been donated this year and winning bidders get to enjoy not only your mouthwatering pies, but a lovely picnic lunch with the entrant whose pie they win at the auction."

Audra looked to Lizzie questioningly. Carter hadn't mentioned anything to her about donating picnic baskets.

Lizzie shrugged. "This is the first I've heard of them auctioning off picnic lunches," she said, keeping her voice low. "Sounds fun, though. Everyone usually just grabs something to eat from one of the food booths."

A slightly balding man with a neatly trimmed, graying beard accepted the microphone from Mrs. Danner. "The good Lord has seen fit to bless us with a mighty fine day for a mighty fine cause. So open your wallets, ladies and gentlemen, and let the picnic lunch bidding begin."

One by one, those half-eaten pies were bid on and won for large amounts of money. Far more than a pie, even fully intact, would ever cost. But it did include a picnic lunch as well. Audra couldn't help but feel touched by the incredibly giving hearts of the community she was now a part of.

Logan was one of the first bidders, bidding on and winning a picnic lunch with Mrs. Simms and her prizewinning pie.

Several more pies were auctioned off and Audra watched the stir of excitement that filled the crowd as bidding on each pie began. Not only were the funds being raised that day going to a good cause, the fund-raiser itself was bringing the community together in wonderful ways.

Audra's only regret was not having thought to give her children spending money with which they could have bid on her pie. Or as it was now—a picnic lunch. That thought had barely surfaced in her mind when she saw Carter set Lily on her feet beside Katie and Mason. A second later, Nathan handed his bidding card to them and the three children, each with a tiny hand placed on the card, raised it up into the air. However, the pie the children were bidding on wasn't hers. Apparently, no one had the heart to bid against the three pint-sized bidders and they won without challenge. Audra looked to Carter, who simply shrugged with a grin. She supposed it all went to the same cause, but it would have been nice to have them bid on her pie. What if no one else wanted it?

Lizzie's pie was the next to be auctioned off. A nice-looking man, who appeared to be closer to Audra's age, stepped to the front of the crowd, his gaze fixed on Lizzie.

"Oh, brother," Lizzie groaned as the man with his wavy blond hair, neatly trimmed goatee and charming grin smiled and then raised his card to start off the bidding.

Audra glanced her way. "What's wrong?" she asked as all attention moved to the auctioneer and the bidding cards going up.

"Anyone but Ryan," her friend muttered.

"Ryan? As in Ryan's Pizza?"

"Ryan's Pies and Pins," her friend replied with a frown. "And, yes, that would be him. He's the older brother of my best friend and used to torment me to no end when we were younger. That is, when he wasn't around his friends acting as if I didn't exist."

"I see," Audra said, her gaze going back to the man who fired up Lizzie's emotions so easily. He certainly wasn't looking at her friend like she didn't exist now.

Much to Lizzie's dismay, Ryan ended up winning her pie, along with the unexpected picnic lunch that was being included in the pie auction that day. "I shouldn't have entered," she mumbled with a frown.

"It can't be that bad," Audra said reassuringly. "Just a friendly picnic lunch surrounded by family and friends."

"That's it," Lizzie said, a smile spreading across her lightly freckled face. "Audra, you're a genius. I'll invite my mother to join Ryan and me for our picnic. That way he'll be forced to behave himself. Because once he gets a closer look at my pie, he'll tease me about my somewhat lacking baking skills."

"I'm sure he won't even notice."

Lizzie fidgeted anxiously with the strawberry-blond ponytail that hung over one slender shoulder. "Not much gets by Ryan. And he has a memory like an elephant. He still hasn't let me forget about the time I burned his toast at the restaurant when I first starting working at Big Dog's."

"Surely he understands that accidents happen."

"He does. Only that wasn't an accident," she confessed with an impish grin.

Audra fought to hold in a giggle. "Why would you do that?"

"Because he's Ryan," Lizzie replied as if that was all the explanation Audra needed.

Before Audra could delve any deeper into Lizzie's reaction to this particular man winning a picnic date with her, she overheard the auctioneer say her name. Glancing around, she saw several hands lift into the air. Mrs. Clark's. Then Rachel Johns's. Followed by a few more hands of men and women she had yet to be introduced to.

Audra smiled nervously as the bidding went on.

"Three hundred dollars," a familiar voice called out. The bid far above any that had been made to that point.

Gasps and whispers moved through the crowd.

"Three hundred dollars?" the auctioneer repeated, no doubt thinking he had misunderstood the far too extravagant bid.

Carter nodded, his determined gaze meeting hers. "One hundred for each of the bakers who put a lot of time and effort into the making of that there delicious-looking pie."

His inclusion of her children in his explanation had emotion flooding her. But three hundred dollars?

"Going once. Going twice…" The eagerly spoken words pulled her back to the moment, her gaze shifting back to the elderly gentleman auctioning off the remainder of her contest pie. "Sold for three hundred dollars!"

Chapter Nine

"Are you crazy?" Audra said as Carter shook out the blue-and-green plaid blanket he'd won along with a food-filled picnic basket in the auction. "Paying that kind of money for a pie you were going to have some of later this evening anyway."

"Crazy about you," he replied, his mouth hitching up on one side in a charming grin. "Now how about we have that lunch I won?"

Crazy about you? Audra's heart did a flip, despite her head's warning that she shouldn't make too much out of his teasing remark. "For the amount you paid," she said as she placed the bright yellow basket atop the blanket Carter had just spread out for their picnic, "you should have gotten all of the picnic lunches."

"Darlin'," he countered as he settled his long

frame atop the blanket, "time spent with you is worth far more than I paid for this here basket."

Blushing at his words, Audra let her gaze fall to the basket as she began unloading the containers of food and placing them on the blanket. "You really are a smooth-talking Texan."

"What I am is a man wanting some time alone with the woman he's come to care a great deal about," he replied as he joined in, pulling out plastic cups, plates and silverware the same vibrant shade of yellow as the basket. "Hence the reason my brother had the kids bid on a basket of their own. That way he can watch over them while you and I enjoy a romantic lunch for two."

"*Romantic* lunch for two?" she said as she sat down next to him on the blanket, trying to keep from melting into his words. Laughing softly, she glanced around them. While it was only the two of them sharing that particular blanket, the grassy area around them was dotted with the blankets of the other auction winners. Not to mention the dozens of other people who were seated on the park's neatly mown lawn, eating food they had purchased from the various food stands.

"Okay, so it's not nearly as private as I might have liked, but I'll just have to make do."

What did he have to say? He sounded so serious. Audra felt a flutter of nerves in the pit of her stomach. Not in the bad sense, but in the sense of her life was about to change direction again.

Carter reached for her hand, twining his fingers through hers. "First, I wanna apologize again for what I tried to do the other night." His teasing tone had grown serious. "My intentions were good, however misguided they were. And while I wanna see my brother and Katie happy I have to admit it would've tangled me all up in knots to wonder what might've been."

"Carter…" she said softly, looking up into his dark, emotion-filled eyes.

"I know you're scared to take a chance when it comes to something more than friendship. I was. But I've come to realize that the risk is one worth taking," he said, running his thumb over the back of her hand. "I'd like to see where things could go between us. And before you answer, I want you to know that I'm fully committed to making this work. For us and for your kids, who've come to mean the world to me."

Suddenly, the moment felt very private. Like it really was only her and Carter sharing that romantic picnic lunch on the park lawn. All she could focus on was Carter's caring gaze and tender tone. "I'd like that, too," she said, emotion tightening her words. "But I have to be honest. I'm not sure I'm ready to open my heart up again completely."

His tender smile never faltered. "So we take baby steps."

She had never met a man so considerate and caring. Could she give Carter what he was hoping for down the road? Her heart. Bradford had crushed it. Just as he had her trust. But Carter was nothing like her ex. He wasn't demanding or selfish. And he cared more deeply for her children than their own father ever had. So as long as she still had a piece of her heart left to build on, no matter how broken or bruised, there was hope for her and Carter to have something more. Something deeper.

Touched by all he'd done to show her how much he truly cared, Audra leaned up and pressed a kiss to his tanned cheek. "Baby steps."

Applause erupted around them, reminding Audra that they weren't alone. She pulled back, her face heating. She couldn't even bring herself to look around.

Carter chuckled. "Should I tell them to hold off on reserving the church, that we're taking things slow?"

"Don't give them any ideas," she muttered past the smile that had moved over her face.

"Let's just eat. We can talk more about us later. When we're away from all the curious stares of at least half the town."

"Sounds like a plan."

Cheeks still flushed with embarrassment, Audra scooped a spoonful of potato salad out onto her plate. "Would you like some?"

"I'm a man, darlin'," he said with a grin. "We rarely turn down food."

She glanced up at him as she emptied a spoonful of the potato salad onto his plate. "Can I ask you something?"

"Anything."

"They said this was the first time there had been picnic lunches going to the winning bidders."

He nodded. "It is."

"And your company donated all the baskets of food?"

He hesitated in replying.

"Cooper Construction didn't buy the picnic items," she answered for him. "You did, didn't you?"

"Reckon it might have been my idea," he admitted with a shrug. "And I might have contributed toward the majority of it. But Nathan pitched in for some of it."

She laughed. "Probably hoping that if everything went as planned for you he wouldn't have to worry about you trying to hand me off to him again."

"Not a chance of that ever happening again," he said, shaking his head. "A real man learns by his mistakes."

"I'm glad to hear it," she teased. "Because you're the only man I'm interested in taking 'baby steps' with."

A firm knock sounded on the office door to Cooper Construction. Then it opened and Rusty Clark poked his graying head inside. "You boys got a minute?"

Nathan looked up from the blueprints he and Carter had been going over and smiled. "Talk about perfect timing," he told the older man with a grin. "We can spare you at least five. We're headed out to look over a new job site in a few."

"This won't take long," the older man assured them as he stepped into the room.

"Have a seat," Carter said from where he stood next to Nathan, motioning to one of the leather armchairs that fronted Nathan's desk.

With a nod, Rusty settled himself into the one closest to the door. "I just got off the phone with the bank and the remainder of the funds for the new recreation center have finally come through. That, along with the money the town has raised through various fund-raisers, will allow us to see our vision for the new center through to completion."

"That's wonderful," Carter said, knowing how hard Rusty had worked to make this happen.

"Indeed," the older man said with a nod. "It was supposed to take another six months or more. So I consider this news a true blessing. My question is, do you think the new recreation center could be ready in time for the town's annual Christmas celebration?"

"Depending on weather conditions during the construction of the building itself, length of time it takes to get the necessary permits and availability of supplies," Carter answered, "I'd say it's possible."

"Blueprints would also need to be drawn up," Nathan added. "Whoever wins the bid for the job will have to be willing to push hard to get the job done in time. But it's definitely doable," Nathan agreed.

"Are you two willing?"

They looked questioningly to Rusty.

"Willing?" Nathan repeated.

"To push to get the job done," he explained. "Because the town council just held an emergency meeting to get the ball rolling on this project. We voted to forgo asking for bids from area contractors to speed things up and in the process will be keeping the work local. Not to mention we'd be using someone we know and trust. A company we know does the utmost quality of work. So my next question is, can you do it?"

"We'd be honored to do the work," Nathan said without hesitation.

Carter nodded. They had other jobs lined up for the next several months, mostly smaller ones. Working around them to build the new recreation center shouldn't be an issue.

"Glad to hear it," Rusty said, a wide smile creasing his weathered cheeks. "The council has decided to dedicate the new center to those we lost in the storm and feel it's only fitting the two of you play an integral part of both the rebuilding of the recreation center and of the dedication ceremony being held before the town's Christmas Eve celebration we'll be holding there if all goes as planned with the building of it."

Carter watched his brother's smile falter and knew the reason for it. Nathan avoided all things Christmas whenever possible. It stirred too many painful memories for him. But he also knew that deep down Nathan needed to do this. Not only to honor Isabel's memory, but also to start to work toward healing emotionally. Katie deserved to grow up in a home filled with both faith and love. Not just love. And she deserved to enjoy the holidays as all children did.

"All the more reason to get the job done on time, if not before," Carter told him. "Isn't that right, Nathan?" he said, giving his brother, who had fallen silent, a nudge.

His brother nodded. "It'll be done in time." There wasn't even a hint of reservation in his brother's declaration.

"I know it will," Rusty replied as he pushed to his feet. "I have every faith you boys can see the job through." Reaching out, he shook their hands. "I'll be in touch to set up a meeting time for us to go over the specifics and get those blueprints started."

"Sounds good." Carter waited until the door closed behind Rusty before looking down at his brother. Tension lined his large frame. "You okay?"

"I will be," his brother said, his words tight with emotion.

"I can run the job without you if you'd rather step back." He hoped for his brother's sake that Nathan wouldn't ask that of him. But he also wasn't going to force him into something he wasn't ready for yet. "I'm sure Rusty would understand."

Nathan pushed his chair away from the desk and stood, striding over to the window to look out. "I already committed to the job and I'd like to think of myself as a man of my word."

"That you are," Carter agreed. His gaze shifted to the clock on the wall. "We'd best get these blueprints rolled up and put away. It's time to head out. We can talk more on the way."

His brother turned from the window and returned to his desk, reaching for the blueprints they'd been going over when Rusty stopped by. Glancing up as he rolled up the stack of papers and inserted them back into their tube, he said, "I'll be there for the dedication, but I won't be staying for the festivities afterward."

"What about Katie?" he asked. "She's gonna want to be there for the Christmas Eve party."

Nathan frowned. "Maybe you or Logan could stay on with her."

His brother needed to be there with his daughter. Katie was old enough now to feel his absence, if only emotionally, during the holidays. "December's a long ways away," Carter said as they started for the door. "Let's hold off on making any plans until the time comes to do so?" In the meantime, he would pray for the

Lord to guide his brother back onto the path he'd been walking on before losing Isabel.

"Are you going to tell me what we're celebrating?" Audra asked with a smile as Mason and Lily ran toward the house, half-eaten, sprinkle-topped, ice-cream cones in hand. Carter had shown up after work that evening, but instead of busying himself with house repairs after dinner he'd announced that he was taking them all out for ice cream to celebrate some big news he'd received that afternoon.

"As soon as we take a seat on your new porch swing. That's where all good talks should take place."

"Is that so?" she said, laughing softly. Her gaze settled onto the bright red swing hanging where the old one had once hung. She'd come home from work to find it there a few days before with a note from Carter telling her he looked forward to spending the coming summer evenings watching the stars with her from that swing. She'd never felt special before, but Carter made her feel that and so much more. This big, strong Texas cowboy, who was both tender and kind with a surprisingly romantic side, was almost too good to be true. But he was real. This romance blossoming between them was real.

"You're dripping."

Audra blinked out of her straying thoughts. "What?"

Grinning, he nodded toward her cone and the streak of chocolate rolling down over her thumb. "Best eat up before it all ends up on your porch," he said as they settled onto the swing.

"I'll eat while you talk," she told him as she wiped her thumb with the napkin she'd had wrapped around her cone. "Now spill," she said as she licked the rest of the melting ice cream away from the cone.

"Rusty Clark stopped by the office today to tell us the council decided to hire Cooper Construction on to build the town's new recreation center."

"Carter!" she exclaimed, throwing her arms around him in what was supposed to be a congratulatory hug, but ended up being a congratulatory kiss instead as he turned to her with a smile. Though it hadn't been planned, the kiss was nice. More than nice, she thought as butterflies took flight in her stomach.

Carter shivered.

Audra was pleased that their first kiss, however unplanned, had affected him every bit as much as it had her. And then she felt it. Cold seeping into the sleeve of her blouse. Not just cold, but wet. The second she processed what the sensation really was, she gasped and pulled away. "Oh, Carter," she groaned. "I'm so sorry."

His gaze dropped to the now empty shell of her ice-cream cone and his grin widened, despite the cold she knew had to be seeping into the back of his flannel shirt. "Darlin'," he began, sounding much more relaxed than a man who'd just had ice cream dumped down his back, "finally getting to kiss you like I'd been wanting to do for a while now was more than worth a little temporary discomfort."

"But your shirt…"

"Can be washed," he replied. "Stop fretting over it."

"How can I when I'm the one whose ice cream you're wearing?" She pushed out of the swing and then turned to him. "Come on."

"Where are we going?"

"To change into something dry and clean," she told him. "We're both sticky messes."

"That we are," he agreed with a grin. "Hold on," he told her as he stood and turned, plucking up the remainder of the fallen blob of chocolate from the seat of the porch swing. Tossing it out into the yard, he used the sleeve of his flannel shirt to wipe the remainder of the melted mess from the seat.

"Carter, your shirt," she blurted out with a frown.

"Is already in need of a wash," he replied. "A little more ice cream isn't gonna make a difference. Besides, we surely wouldn't want an army of ants to commandeer our little front porch hideaway."

"I hadn't considered that," she replied. "But now that you mention it, I wouldn't want those pesky little insects to commandeer you, either. So let's go inside so you can get cleaned up. You can use the downstairs guest bathroom." One the previous owners had added on just off the kitchen years before. And thankfully so. Most of the older homes, like hers, only had one upstairs bathroom. "I'll run upstairs and change," she said, holding out her arm to show him where the back of her sleeve had a large, sticky stain. "Then I need to make sure the kids are getting ready for bed like I told them to."

He nodded. "Sounds like a plan."

"I'll lend you a T-shirt to wear home tonight. Leave yours in the bathroom and I'll throw it into the wash before I go to bed." It was the least she could do, seeing as how she had made a mess of his clean flannel shirt and no doubt the T-shirt he wore underneath.

He chuckled. "I doubt you're gonna have anything that'll fit me."

"Oh ye of little faith," she teased as they stepped inside. "Be right back," she told him as she hurried up the stairs to get him that shirt she'd promised him. She returned, handing him the neatly folded red bundle. "Here you go," she said with a smile.

"Appreciate it," he drawled.

"It was either this one or a tie-dyed sleep shirt with bright yellow smiley faces all over it. They were the only shirts I had that might be large enough to fit those broad shoulders of yours."

"Good choice," he said, without even looking to see what she'd chosen for him instead.

She smiled, hoping that he'd feel the same way once he put on the red T-shirt. "I won't be long," she said and then hurried back up the stairs to see to her children.

"I'll wait for you on the porch," he called after her.

Ten minutes or so later when Audra came back down the stairs expecting Carter to be outside, she found him waiting for her in the entryway instead. Muscular arms folded in front of his wide chest, one dark brow lifting as the faintest hint of a smile played at the corners of his mouth. "A snowman?"

She bought a hand to her mouth to muffle the snicker that slipped past her lips as she took in the sight of Carter dressed in the oversize men's T-shirt she sometimes wore with leggings when lounging around the house. The bright red T-shirt, at least a size too small, molded to his broad shoulders and muscular chest in a way most women would appreciate. But it was the snowman part that made her smile. Starting just below the slight dip of the crew neck down to a mere two or three inches from the shirt's hem, two stacked snowballs were imprinted on the shirt's front. Three black buttons ran down the slightly smaller snowball on top while two spindly twigs poked out from either side of it. The makeshift arms stretched up and out across the tops of the sleeves in a curling, whimsical manner.

"I've gone from the heroic Lone Ranger to Frosty the Snowman."

Her gaze lifted from the stacked snowballs to connect with his and her smile widened. "I have to admit you're the most adorable snowman I've ever laid eyes on."

"I think I'd prefer to be wearing that shoe-polish mask."

"I might have some shoe polish upstairs," she teased. "If you'd prefer, we could put some around your eyes and make you the Lone Snowman…"

Reaching out, he drew her to him, folding his

arms around her waist. "Not a chance." Then, not by accident this time, he lowered his mouth to hers in a sweet kiss.

Audra melted against him with a sigh.

"Mommy?" Lily called out from the top of the stairs. "Are you coming to tuck us in?"

Both she and Carter parted instantly, their gazes locked. "They were hoping you would come upstairs with me to tell them good-night," she explained in a guilty whisper. "I was going to ask you, but got sidetracked when I saw you standing here. You don't have to, though," she quickly added, knowing her ex-husband had wanted nothing to do with their children's bed-time rituals.

"There is no 'have to' about it," he assured her. "I'd be happy to." He looked toward the top of the stairs, calling out in response to Lily's sleepy plea, "Your momma and I are on our way up right now."

"Yay!" The sound of Lily's tiny feet pattering excitedly down the upstairs hall echoed in the stairwell, making Audra smile. Her children adored Carter. She adored Carter. Looking up at him, she said, "Are you sure you don't mind doing this?"

"I don't mind at all," he said, reaching for her hand. "In fact, I happen to be a very good 'tucker-in-er.' Just ask my niece."

She gave his hand a grateful squeeze as they made their way up the stairs together. Then she said a quick prayer of thanks to the good Lord for bringing Carter into their lives.

They stopped by Lily's room first. The second her daughter saw him step into the open doorway, her tiny face lit up.

"I heard someone was asking for me," he said with a grin.

Her daughter nodded. Then her gaze dropped down to the front of the T-shirt Audra had loaned him. "My mommy has a shirt like that. But hers is a lady snowman."

Carter glanced Audra's direction, that dark brow of his shooting upward once again.

"Honey," Audra said, unable to keep the mirth from her voice, "it only looked like a lady snowman because Mommy was wearing it. Now it's a very manly snowman. Mr. Cooper is borrowing Mommy's shirt because I accidentally spilled some of my ice-cream cone on the one he was wearing tonight."

"Some?" Carter muttered beside her with a grin.

"Okay," Audra conceded. "Most."

Lily studied Carter curiously. "You should have a carrot nose."

He chuckled. "And have bunnies hopping after me, trying to nibble at it?"

Lily snorted. "You're too tall for a bunny to nibble on your nose. But if you were crawling on the ground—"

"All right, young lady," Audra said, cutting off her daughter's endless chatter. "Time for you to get to sleep. You and Mr. Cooper can discuss bunnies and carrot noses tomorrow."

"Okay," she said with a yawn, her adoring gaze fixed on Carter. "Are you going to tuck me in?"

"We can't very well have you rolling out of bed if I don't," he teased as he stepped up to the bed and began tucking the pink floral quilt under her from neck to toes.

Lily giggled.

"There you go," Carter said, taking a step back to survey his handiwork. "Snug as a bug."

"How am I supposed to hug you good-night with my arms tucked in?" her daughter asked with a pout.

Audra stood back, watching the interaction between Carter and her daughter. He was so good with Lily. But then he'd had Katie to practice on. It was clear he absolutely adored his young niece.

Carter pretended to mull over Lily's question. "I suppose I could try to sew a couple of arm holes in the quilt for you to slip your arms through. Then you'd be able to hug me."

"You can't do that," her daughter said with another giggle. "You just need to let my arms out."

"That might work, too," he said with a nod as he loosened the blanket along her sides. "Sure enough," he acknowledged as she slipped her arms free of the quilt. "How did you become such a smart little girl?"

Her daughter soaked up his praise like a wilting flower finally receiving some much-needed rain. That thought gave Audra a moment of pause. Would her daughter wilt again once Carter was ready to move on? Because he wasn't the settling-down type. He'd been honest with her about that from the very beginning. That meant keeping her heart tucked in every bit as firmly as Lily had been beneath the covers.

After a quick bedtime prayer, Audra kissed Lily good-night. Then Carter leaned in for a hug, wishing her daughter sweet dreams. They closed the door behind them as they moved farther down the hall to Mason's room.

Mason tried not to appear overly excited about Carter's coming in to wish him good-night, but Audra knew better. "Didn't you have something you wanted to say to Mr. Cooper?"

Her son's gaze lowered to the shirt. "Why are you wearing that snowman shirt?"

"I'm wondering that same thing myself," Carter replied with a husky chuckle.

"I wasn't referring to the shirt," Audra told her son.

"Thank you for taking us to get ice cream," Mason said, looking up at him from where he lay in his bed.

Carter gave a nod. "Maybe we can do it again sometime."

"Maybe Katie could go with us."

"She'd like that. Mighty nice of you to think of asking her to join us." His gaze moved over the chocolate-brown comforter her son had drawn up as far as his tiny chest. "I just tucked your sister in. You need me to tuck you in, too?"

Her son shook his head. "I'm too old to be tucked in," he said, his gaze straying in her direction, as if begging her not to tell Carter that she usually did so with him every night anyway.

"I see," Carter replied. "Reckon I should have figured as much, seeing as how you're the man of this here house."

"It's late," Audra said, cutting in. "Time to say your prayers and then get to sleep. You have school tomorrow."

When the prayer ended, Audra kissed her

son's brow and then turned to walk with Carter out of the room.

"Mr. Cooper..." her son called out.

Carter paused in the doorway, turning with a warm smile. "Yes, son?"

"A hug good-night would be okay, I suppose."

Audra's heart lurched and her eyes stung with unshed tears as Carter crossed the room without hesitation to give her son the hug that he'd asked for. Mason had been so withdrawn at the end from his own father and understandably so. A boy's affection could only be pushed away so many times before he shut off and stopped offering it. That her son trusted Carter enough to allow himself to be vulnerable to possibly more of the same rejection he'd suffered with his father touched her so very deeply. The burn of unshed tears had her slipping out into the hall as Audra tried to collect herself.

Carter stepped from the room, closing the door behind him. "Audra?"

She took a deep breath, fanning at her tear-filled eyes. "I just need a moment."

He closed the distance between them and caught her face between his hands, tilting it upward. "Darlin'," he said with a sigh, "why the tears?"

"They aren't precisely tears yet," she countered, embarrassed by her inability to control her emotions. "They have to fall first."

"Well, if you're gonna cry, we'd best go fetch that bucket you were using under your leaky sink. I know how much water your pretty eyes can put out when they have a mind to."

His teasing words, no matter how true, had her laughing. "I really am doing my best to refrain from flooding the hallway, but you sure don't make it easy." She grew serious then. "Thank you for being so good to my children."

There was such tenderness in his eyes as he looked down at her. "I know how hard it must be for you to trust another man not to hurt them the way your husband did. And I thank you for placing your trust in me and allowing me to be a part of their lives." He pressed a kiss to the tip of her nose before letting his hands fall away. "Come on, darlin'. Let's go spend a few more minutes enjoying the stars. Then I'd best head home."

Nodding, she turned and started for the stairs. "I'm still waiting to discover that you're not as perfect as you appear to be," she said over her shoulder with a smile as she made her way downstairs.

"Ah, but maybe that is my imperfection," he replied as he reached past her to hold the screen door open for her. "I'm too perfect."

Laughing softly, she stepped outside, shaking her head. She loved the playful, teasing side of Carter. "So tell me more about the rec center job," Audra said as she settled onto the swing.

He nodded with a grin. "Nathan and I figured we had a shot at the job, but normally these things have to go up for bid with several contractors. Braxton's town council decided to forgo bringing in estimates from other contractors and go with Cooper Construction because we're local and they know the quality of work we've done around town in the past."

She smiled up at him. "I'm so happy for you and Nathan. From what I've heard, it's going to be a really big job." The new rec center possibly having a large indoor swimming pool and a basketball court among other amenities.

"It will be, meaning it's going to take up a pretty big chunk of our time on occasion," he said, looking uneasy about having to tell her that.

"Of course it will," she said, wanting him to know she understood. "This is what you do. I'm sure there will be times when certain jobs demand more of your time than others do."

"And that's not a problem for you?"

"I feel blessed for any time that I get to spend with you," she answered honestly.

"I feel the same way." He wrapped an arm around her shoulders, drawing her near.

It was a beautiful, clear night. The air cool and crisp. A calming silence settled in the land around them. There they sat in comfortable silence for several long minutes, looking out at the stars that dotted the wide, cloudless Texas night sky.

"Audra…"

"Hmm?" she murmured as she snuggled into the warmth of his side.

"I'd like to get your kids a dog."

His announcement came from out of the blue. "A dog?" she repeated, lifting her head to look up at him.

"I was thinking that they might like having one," he explained. "There's plenty of room out here for one to run. And a dog's real good at knowing when someone needs a little extra affection."

As Carter himself was so good at. He always knew when she needed someone to talk to or a shoulder to lean on. Or, as it seemed to be the case with her, one to cry on. "A dog is a big responsibility," she said as she considered his suggestion.

"Mostly during the training of it, which I would help with," he replied. "And there are plenty more pluses to having a dog. He'd keep pesky little critters like raccoons away from the house. He'd bark to let you know when you have company. He'd be excited to see you and the kids every time you came home. And, most importantly," he added, "I really think Mason and Lily would take to the idea of having their very own dog to love and care for."

"I know they would," she answered with a smile, determined not to cry as she sat looking up into his kind, thoughtful eyes. If she hadn't been falling for him already, Audra would have done so right then and there. As it was, she'd just fallen a little bit harder.

Chapter Ten

"You ready to go?" Carter asked as he stood at the foot of the front porch steps. Above, on the roof, his brothers continued to work on repairs as they had been doing since shortly after daybreak that morning.

Audra hesitated with a glance back toward the door. "Maybe we should take the children with us." She turned back to him with a worried frown. "Lily likes to pick out the flowers."

"I'm sure we'll be needing to make more than one trip to the nursery," he said, hoping they could get a move on before the kids did take notice and ask to go with them. If that were the case, the surprise he had planned for that afternoon would no longer be a surprise. "Besides, they just started watching that princess movie. We'll be back before they know it."

Laughing softly, she made her way down the

steps to join him. "Beauty isn't a princess. At least, not until she marries the beast."

His eyes rounded. "She marries the bull?"

"The bull is actually a prince that's been changed into a beast. He can only change back into his princely form by learning to love and to be loved back in return."

As he walked her out to the truck, Carter said, "Who knew movies for little kids could be so complicated? Logan never made mention of it. He's the one who usually does the movie watching with Katie. I'm the ball-tosser and tea-party participant."

Audra waved to his brothers, who paused in their work and waved back, and Carter pulled away. "I feel bad leaving while they're up on that hot roof working."

He offered a reassuring smile. "We're Texans, darlin'. And like our state's plant, the prickly pear cactus, we're tough. The good Lord put us here in Texas because we thrive in the heat."

They drove to Hope's Garden, the local nursery where Logan purchased most of his landscaping plants and trees for his business. They were greeted by Jack Dillan, who had been close friends with Carter's daddy, both men having high hopes at one point that Logan and Jack's daughter, Hope, would merge the two families. But things hadn't worked out and Hope had moved to San Diego after college.

"I was wondering if you were gonna make it by today," Jack said, extending a hand in greeting. His keen gaze shifted to Audra. "This must be the pretty little filly you were telling me about."

Carter couldn't help but smile as he watched the blush move across her face. "Jack Dillan, I'd like you to meet Audra Marshall. She bought the old Harris place and is looking to brighten it up with some real pretty flowers."

"Ms. Marshall," the older man greeted with a widening grin.

"It's a pleasure to meet you," she said.

"Come on into the greenhouse," he said with a wave as he started off toward the arched, multiwindowed building. "We've got plenty of colorful posies for you to choose from."

"I'll grab a cart while you start making your selections," Carter told her.

Nodding, Audra let Jack take her along the aisles, showing her the large selection of flowers he carried.

Carter wheeled the narrow metal cart back to where Audra had selected several containers of dark pink-and-white-striped phlox. "Good choice," he said as he began loading the plastic flower-filled planters onto the top tray of the nursery's shopping cart. He just hoped that Audra was happy with the choice he'd made a few days before on her behalf.

After what felt like forever, mostly due to his eagerness to show Audra the pup he'd chosen for Mason and Lily from among the several he and Audra had looked at during their trip to the pound, they loaded up her flower garden selections and then went to pay.

"Got everything you need?" Jack asked as he rung her out.

"I think so," she said as she placed her wallet back into her purse.

"I think we might be missing one more thing," Carter announced from behind her.

She turned to him questioningly.

He looked past her to the older man. "Jack."

"Be right back," he said with a beaming smile. He left, returning a few moments later with the adorable little, droopy-eared bloodhound mix Carter and Audra had been especially taken with when they'd gone to the pound earlier in the week. "Can't have you forgetting this little guy," Jack said as he set the squirming pup down onto the greenhouse floor and handed Carter the loop end of the leash that was attached to him.

"Carter," Audra gasped as she sank to her knees to fawn over the excited mutt.

He smiled at her reaction. "You seemed mighty taken with him, so I figured if you liked him the kids would, too. I went back and filled out the application to adopt him that same day but couldn't pick him up until this morning once all of his shots had been done and he'd been fixed. So I called and asked Jack if he'd mind my dropping this little guy off and keeping him here until you and I could pick him up and take him home to the kids together."

She glanced up at him, her eyes misting over with what he hoped was happiness. "So he's ours now?"

The pup, taking advantage of Audra's momentary distraction, jumped up to plant a wet kiss on her cheek.

Jack chuckled. "Appears he thinks so."

Carter nodded. "He's all yours." *I'm all yours.* He kept those words to himself, knowing he wanted everything to be right when he made that heartfelt declaration to Audra. And for things to be right he needed to remove the guilt of having kept the truth from his brother. That meant having that talk with Nathan that he'd been trying to work himself up to having. Then maybe that part of him that had been tied up emotionally for the past year and a half would finally be free to love without guilt or reservation.

Audra scooped the pup up in her arms and stood. "Mason and Lily are going to love him to pieces. I know I already do and he's only been mine for a few minutes."

The joy on her face filled him with such pleasure. Carter turned to Jack. "Thanks for keeping an eye on this little one for a spell and for helping me surprise Audra."

She looked at Jack. "Yes, thank you so much. For both the dog-sitting and for your help in choosing from all your beautiful annuals. I will be back."

Jack smiled. "I hope you will."

"We'd best get going," Carter said, slipping an arm around her waist. "We've got us some kids to surprise."

His brothers were seated on the front porch steps, taking what looked to be a water break, when Carter pulled up the drive. "No sign of the children," he said to Audra, who sat beside him, holding the newest addition to her family securely in her arms.

"Unless your brothers are keeping them corralled inside." She looked his way. "Were they in on this surprise, too?"

"Nope," he said with a grin as he shut off the engine. "Figured I'd just let them think we picked him out together. Can't have them thinking I'm a softie or anything."

She laughed. "You are a softie, Carter Cooper. You might as well accept that as a fact and move on."

"You trying to ruin my manly Texas cowboy reputation?" he teased as he stepped from the truck. Rounding the front, he opened the passenger door to take the pup from Audra's lap and lowered it to the ground.

"In answer to your question," she said as Carter handed her the leather loop at the end of the leash he'd picked up the day he went to get the pooch from the pound, "I happen to find big, strong men who join in tea parties and can braid my daughter's hair far more manly than those men who would never ever consider doing those kinds of things."

He gave a husky chuckle. "Reckon I have Katie to thank for a good part of my manliness, then."

"Can't say I recall ever seeing flowers at Hope's Garden that come with fur and a tail," Logan called out from his perch on the porch.

"Maybe it's some sort of fancy new hybrid posy," Nathan added with a grin.

"*He* happens to be a surprise," Carter grumbled, trying to keep his voice low. His gaze moved past his brothers as the screen door swung open and three shrieking little ones flew out of the house.

"Whose doggy is that?" Lily exclaimed as she raced after her brother and Katie.

Audra knelt in the grass, holding onto the pup's leash. "He's yours," she told Lily with a beaming smile.

"Ours?" Mason gasped as he dropped onto his knees beside his mother.

The pup pounced on him, trying his hardest to cover Mason's face in wet, puppy kisses. But her son managed to dodge most of them, giggling as he did so.

"Yes," Audra told her. "Ours."

Carter stood back, watching as Lily practically fell atop the dog in her eagerness to give it a hug.

Katie joined in, scratching the dog's ears. The pup alternated between trying to kiss her and then Mason.

"From the look of things," Nathan muttered as he and Logan moved to stand beside Carter in the yard, "I'd say you just snagged yourself another piece of her heart."

He prayed that was the case. Funny thing was if anyone had told him that day when he'd gotten sidetracked on his way into town that his determination to remain a bachelor was going to disappear as fast as his momma's cranberry stuffing used to at Thanksgiving dinners, he would have told them they were plumb crazy. Now it was him who was crazy—about Audra. He sent up a silent prayer of thanks to the good Lord for bringing Audra and her children into his life. Audra's laughter filled the air as the pup scampered playfully around her legs, long ears flopping about.

"That's my intention," Carter replied as he moved to join into the fracas. He walked up to Audra, slipping his hand around her slender waist. "Appears I've got myself some competition for your smiles."

"No worry," she said, smiling up at him. "I've got plenty to go around."

The pup stopped playing to sniff at the ground. A second later, he took off, jerking the leash right out of Audra's grasp, dragging its leash behind it.

"Where's he going?" Lily asked, disappointed that their new friend had stopped playing.

"He's going toward the bushes," Mason said, pointing to the cluster of shrubs at the corner of the house.

"Looks to me like he's picked up a scent," Logan said as the bundle of fur sniffed its way across the yard like a pup on a mission.

"He's part coonhound," Carter explained. "They're known for their hunting skills and they're real good at tracking things down."

The pup disappeared into the bushes in a series of excited yaps. A few seconds later, a rather annoyed looking armadillo scurried out from under one of the bushes as fast as its nearly nonexistent legs could carry it.

"Look what he found!" Lily exclaimed.

The pup darted in wide circles about the fleeing critter, clearly wanting to play. Chuckling, Carter went to fetch it back, giving the poor startled animal a chance to make good on its escape. Not that it would have harmed the armadillo. The pup had simply wanted to play and had chosen an unwilling playmate.

"Here you go," Carter said, handing control of the leash over to Mason.

Mason settled onto the ground to hug the pup again. "Good job, Boone!"

"Boone?" Audra repeated as Lily and Katie moved in to smother the pup in even more affection.

Her son looked up from the tangle of pup and children to smile at her. "Like Daniel Boone," he said as if his momma should have known where he'd pulled the name from. "He was a good tracker, too."

"I'd say that's a right good choice for a name," Nathan said with a nod.

"He wore an animal on his head," Lily announced.

Carter and his brothers attempted to smother their laughter.

"Reckon you could say that," Logan said with a grin.

"We've read a few books about Daniel Boone," Audra explained with a hint of a blush.

"I gathered as much," Carter said with a chuckle.

"We'd best get back to work on that roof if we're gonna be finished up in time for supper," Nathan announced, starting for the ladder they had secured against the side of the house.

Logan followed.

"I'll be up in a minute," Carter called after them. "I'm gonna grab the flats of flowers from the back of the truck."

"I'll help you," Audra said and then turned to the children just as Boone tackled Katie, taking her from a sitting position to lying flat on her back on the ground. She gasped, fearing that in his exuberance, the pup might have hurt her, but Katie popped back upright with a giggle. Relief swept through her. "Can you kids keep an eye on Boone while I help Carter get the flowers and then go inside and start cooking?"

"We sure can," Katie replied as the dog circled around them, yipping loudly.

"We'll take good care of him," Lily answered as she stretched out on the ground next to Katie, no doubt seeking some of the pup's attention.

Mason, who stood holding onto the leash, nodded in agreement.

"You need any help with the cooking?" Carter asked.

Audra turned to look up at him with that pretty smile of hers. "I think I can handle it. Besides, you can't very well leave your brothers to do all the work while you stay inside and sneak tastes of all the picnic foods."

"Wanna bet?" he said with a grin. "Darlin', when it comes to your pecan pie, I'd put on one of them frilly little aprons of yours and offer to wash all the dishes for a sneak taste of it." Audra had invited them all to stay for a cookout, complete with barbecued baked beans, potato salad and his favorite—pecan pie. He had no doubt he and his brothers would have her roof repairs completed in plenty of time. The promise of a home-cooked meal gave a man plenty of incentive to work hard.

She laughed. "Tempting as your offer is, because I can't imagine you strutting around my kitchen in a frilly apron, you need to stay out here and help your brothers."

"Reckon you're right," he agreed. "I best get back to work."

"See you after a bit," she said.

If they weren't surrounded by others, he'd lean in and give her a sweet kiss. As it was, he settled for a nod and then turned and strode around the side of the house, where the roofing supplies had been placed.

The men's voices drifted in through the open kitchen window. They worked so well together. Playful taunts and brotherly chatter made Audra long for what she would never have—siblings. She was so thankful to God for giving her another child. She had begun to think she might never conceive again after Mason. But the Lord had blessed her with her beautiful baby girl. Now her children would always have somebody in their life to lean on, to share their ups and downs with, and to love.

Pie in the oven, she walked over to the phone and dialed Mildred Timmons's number. Millie was part of the Cooper family and such a kind woman. She should be at their cookout as well if she didn't already have plans for supper.

"Hello?" the older woman said cheerily as she answered the call.

"Millie, it's Audra Marshall."

"Well, hello, dear."

"I was calling to invite you to a cookout. Carter and his brothers are here working on my roof and Katie is playing with the kids. We'll probably start grilling out around four thirty and we'd love to have you join us."

"Aren't you a sweetheart," Millie replied. "I would love to come. What can I bring?"

"There's no need to bring anything. We have plenty of food," Audra assured her. "Unless you don't care for chicken. That's what we're grilling out."

"Chicken is fine. But I insist on bringing something. How about I whip up some of my sweet corn bread and bring it?"

"That sounds delicious," Audra said. "I'm so glad you can come."

"I appreciate the invitation," Millie replied. "It gets a mite lonely out here sometimes. That's why I love watching little Katie for Nathan. She's such a joy to be around."

"I'm sure it does," Audra said. "And I couldn't agree more about Katie. My children and I adore her."

"And she adores you and your children," Millie said. "It's practically all she talks about when she's here. Anyhow, I'll let you go and we'll see you in a couple hours."

"See you then."

Audra returned the phone to its cradle and

then went to check on the potatoes she had left boiling on the stove when she'd made her call.

An hour later, the cooking was done. Carter's very favorite pecan pie was in the oven and the dishes were washed and set out to dry. Grabbing the stack of colorful plastic picnic plates from the table and the basket of plastic silverware, she went outside to check on the kids and start the grill.

The front yard was empty. Stepping off the porch, she looked around and was about to call out when a very deep male voice called down, "They're around back."

Turning, she shielded her eyes from the sun with a hand as she looked up at the porch roof. Nathan was seated there, taking a drink from a water bottle. She smiled up at him. "How's it going?"

"Almost done with repairs. They should hold until you're able to put a new roof on."

Logan came around the corner with a wheelbarrow and smiled in greeting. "Cleanup time," he said as he began picking up the broken shingles they'd removed from her roof and tossed to the ground.

"I really appreciate everything you all have done for us." They'd spent their day off working on her house when they could have been doing something so much more enjoyable.

"We're glad to help out," Nathan said.

Logan agreed with a nod of his dark head.

Audra glanced around. "Where's your brother?"

Logan tossed several pieces of slate into the wheelbarrow. "He's replacing a couple of missing slates on the back porch roof. Headed back there after the kids wandered back that way with the dog. Said he wanted to keep an eye on them."

"I wouldn't be surprised if you found him in the yard playing, too," Nathan muttered as he tossed the empty water bottle into the wheelbarrow below. "My brother tends to be a big kid himself when he's around those of a like mind."

Smiling, Audra nodded. "I've noticed. That's what I love most about him. His willingness to be playful and join in."

Nathan's dark brow lifted. "Love?" he drawled.

"Excuse me?" she replied in confusion.

"You said that's what you love about him," Logan said, grinning from ear to ear.

She had? Oh, dear...

Carter's younger brother chuckled. "No worries. Your secret's safe with us."

Heat filled her cheeks. "It's not that way. I mean, I like your brother. A lot. But he's not looking...I mean I don't want..." She sighed. "I should go check on the children."

Audra hurried away, shocked that she'd used

the word *love* in reference to Carter. Even if it was only in regards to his playful side. She hesitated in her step, realizing that if she were honest with herself it wasn't only his playful side she loved. It was his smile. His deep faith in the Lord. His compassion for others. His thoughtfulness. It was suddenly hard to draw breath. How had she allowed this to happen? She'd fallen in love with Carter Cooper.

Before she could digest that last thought, Boone raced past her, three giggling children following behind.

Carter's husky laughter drifted down from the back porch roof.

Gathering her courage, Audra stepped around the corner of the house. "Have they been chasing after him since I went inside?"

Carter's handsome face peered over the edge of the roof. "Pretty much."

She turned, watching the comical sight of her children and Katie, even with her limp, trailing after the pup, whose bright blue leash was skimming over the grass behind it. Laughter spilled from her lips. "I'll be amazed if they can stay awake through dinner with all the energy they've been exerting."

A long leg swung down from the roof, its booted foot settling onto one of the ladder rungs, immediately followed by the other as he worked his way down to where she stood watching him.

"You didn't have to stop on account of me," she said, unable to look him in the eye, knowing that her heart was determined to lead her to what would eventually be more heartache.

"I didn't. You just happen to have perfect timing. I'm all done up there." He leaned in, studying her face. "Everything okay?"

"Yes," she said, wishing her racing heart would slow. *She loved him.* "I was just coming out to check on the kids and light the grill. I should go do that."

Reaching out, he took the stack of plates and silverware from her. "I'll set the table and fire up the grill."

"You don't have to do that," she said, chasing after him as he started for the grill they'd placed on the small brick patio Carter had put in for her a few steps away from her back porch. The only other thing on the patio was a wooden picnic table with attached bench seats. Perfect for cookouts.

"I want to," he said as he doled out the plates along each side of the long wooden table. Then he stepped up to the grill and raised its lid. "I happen to enjoy grilling out."

Bradford had liked grilling out, too. Until

he grew bored with it. Just as he had her. How long would it take Carter to tire of her?

"Audra, I can tell something's bothering you," Carter said with a sigh of frustration. "Talk to me, darlin'."

"Hello…"

They turned as Mildred Timmons rounded the corner of the house.

"Millie?" Carter said in surprise as he strode over to greet the older woman with a welcoming hug.

"I asked Millie to join us for our cookout," Audra explained, grateful for the older woman's timing. She wasn't ready to talk to Carter about what was bothering her. How could she? The man wasn't looking for love. And she wasn't looking to give her heart away again only to have it rejected. Once had been hard enough. But something told her that with Carter it would be beyond heartbreaking. She managed a smile for the older woman as she moved to join them. "I'm so glad you were able to make it."

"I set the corn bread on the stove. The boys told me I'd find you out back." Her gaze drifted across the yard to where all three children and the pup were lying atop the grass, worn out from their running about. "Looks like there's been an addition to the family."

"That's Boone," Audra told her, her smile

widening, despite her inner turmoil, as she watched Lily sit up and lean over to hug the dog beside her. Seeing her children so joyful, so completely taken by the overly affectionate pup, she felt such a deep sense of regret for not standing up to Bradford all those times he'd refused their pleas for a pet of their own. "Carter surprised us with him today. He's beyond adorable and the kids are thrilled to have a dog of their very own. Their father was never big on animals." She couldn't keep the edge of sadness from her voice as she spoke.

"Well, he doesn't know what he's missing," Millie said empathetically. "The good Lord gave sweet pups like that the ability to love those who love them back and to watch over those they care about." She looked up at Carter. "Appears to me our Audra here has found herself a smart man this time around."

"Millie," Carter muttered, looking to Audra as if he feared she might be offended by the older woman's bluntness.

"No need to get your britches in a twist, young man. All I'm saying is that a woman knows a surefire way to a man's heart is through her cooking. But few men realize that one way to a woman's heart is with a puppy. Especially one that fills her children with such tremendous joy."

He met Audra's gaze. "My intention was to give Mason and Lily something that I knew from my own childhood would give them unconditional love. If I succeeded in accomplishing more by doing so, I will count myself a very blessed man, as well." Turning back to Millie, he said, "I'll leave you two ladies to visit while I go get washed up."

Audra watched him go, longing in her heart.

"He cares for you a great deal," Millie said beside her.

Tears stung Audra's eyes. "I can't do this again."

"Do what, dear?"

"Love a man who might never love me back," she said.

"What makes you think Carter couldn't love you back?"

Turning to Millie, she said sadly, "Because he's not looking for anything long-term. And because it would be just punishment for me breaking the vows I spoke before God when I married Bradford. I pledged in church to stay with my husband until death do us part, but I was the one to file for divorce and end my marriage."

"Honey, let's have us a seat over at the picnic table," Millie suggested, her kind, caring tone reminding Audra of the many talks she'd had with her own mother. "I'd like to talk to you."

Nodding and doing her best not to give in to the tears, she followed Millie over to the brick patio. Once they were seated, the older woman reached across to take her hand.

"You seem to be a woman who loves deeply and feels her losses every bit as deeply. Carter told me a little about your ex-husband and about the loss of your parents when you were such a tender age. I'm sorry you've had to go through so much heartache. Now I'm gonna tell you what I would've told my daughter if I'd had one. God isn't looking to punish you for ending your marriage. From what I understand, you tried with everything you had in you to make it work. But, sweetie," she said, giving Audra's hand a squeeze, "no one, not you, not I, not our wondrous Lord above, can help a sinner if he or she refuses to be helped. In the end, you did what you needed to do to protect your little ones. God understands that."

Millie's words surprisingly helped to ease some of Audra's long-harbored guilt where her failed marriage was concerned. Sniffing softly, she lifted her gaze from the table to meet the kind woman's gaze. "Thank you for saying that. I guess I felt so guilty about ending my marriage, no matter how awful it had become, that

I never considered God might not lay the blame for it at my feet."

"Have you forgiven your ex-husband for his failings?"

Audra thought about it for a long moment and then shook her head. "I don't believe I have."

"It might help you to move on. Forgiveness has the ability to heal the heart, you know."

She was right. It was time to move on, and to do so she needed to forgive Bradford his trespasses and pray he found the help he needed to become the Christian he once was. "I can do that," she said determinedly.

"Now that we've got that put to rights, I wanna talk to you about Carter. With no family of my own, they've become my boys and I love them with all my heart."

"I've seen that," Audra said with a soft smile.

"When Nathan lost Isabel, all three of them boys pulled back from serious relationships of any kind. They were still feeling the loss of those they loved and scared to ever intentionally put their hearts at risk of losing someone they love ever again. But fears fade and hearts tend to have a mind of their own. I know my Carter and he feels deeply for you. Give him a chance to prove it to you. He's not your ex."

"I want to," she said on a choked sob.

"Then do so," Millie said simply. "Let your heart guide you to the happiness you deserve."

She had trusted her heart once, but looking back now she knew that what she'd thought had been love hadn't even been close to the feelings she had for Carter. Audra nodded. "I prayed for the Lord to guide me down the right path, unsure if he would listen because of my walking away from my marriage. But He did listen. He brought a wonderful, caring man into my life." She glanced toward her children and her smile returned. "Our lives. He's given me a second chance at finding what my heart's been searching for. And now I know what I need to do to finally move on and trust in what Carter and I have."

Millie nodded, a huge smile lighting her face. "Thatta girl. Glad to know Carter has the right of it."

She looked questioningly at Millie.

"That boy's gone and found himself a real good woman."

Chapter Eleven

Carter kept a firm grip on the wheel as he drove to Nathan's place, his thoughts both on Audra and of what he needed to do. He hadn't expected to fall for the pretty little mother of two, but he had. Hard. God had brought them into his life for a reason. To take his lonely, closed-off heart and fill it with warmth and love. And to guide him on a better path. One free of protective secrets and guilt over choices he'd made.

Nathan's truck was outside, but then he was usually home on a Sunday afternoon. Pulling up to the house, Carter cut the engine and stepped out, heart pounding. Closing the door, he made his way toward his brother's front porch.

Before he could reach it, Nathan stepped around the side of the house, hammer in hand.

"Thought I heard someone pull up. I was out back hammering down a few nails that pulled loose in Katie's playhouse. She and her dolls are having a tea party and she didn't want them to accidentally catch their dresses on one of the lifted nail heads."

Carter nodded. "So Katie's out back?"

Nathan paused to study him before replying, "In her playhouse, yes. What's wrong?"

"Can we step inside?" He didn't want to risk Katie coming around the house and overhearing their conversation.

Concern lit his brother's face. "Sure. Come on in." He led Carter into the house. "Living room work?"

"Yes."

"Can I get you something to drink?" his brother asked as Carter took a seat on the sofa. "Lemonade? Glass of ice water?"

"No, thanks," Carter replied with a troubled frown.

Nathan sank into the recliner chair across from him. "You and Audra have a falling-out?"

Carter's gaze lifted to meet his brother's. "Audra?"

"Can't think of anything else that would set you in this mood."

"Audra and I are fine."

"You know," his brother said, "there was a

time when you would have run the other way when it came to falling in love, but after getting to know Audra and her kids, seeing how you spark to life when you're around them, I can understand why you're running head-on toward the happiness you could have with them."

Happiness like his brother had once had for himself.

"You should tell her you love her," Nathan said.

"I intend to," he said. "But first there's something I need to tell you."

"Me?"

"It's about Isabel," he said, sounding much calmer than he felt inside.

Nathan's entire body went rigid. "What about her?"

Carter's gut churned. "That day when I found her," he began, hot tears welling in his dark eyes, "she was still breathing."

"What?" The word cracked like an icy river during a spring thaw.

"She was buried under debris and barely conscious," Carter went on, fearing he would lose the courage to reach back to that horrible moment in his mind. "I couldn't free her, so I took off my jacket and leaned over her to protect her from the cold rain that was still falling. She took my hand in her weak grasp and

I told her she was gonna be all right. But even with all the first-aid training I'd had, I couldn't help her."

"Why didn't you come find me?" Nathan demanded, pushing up from the recliner.

Through tear-blurred eyes, he watched as his brother went to stand at the window, his broad shoulders shuddering with tears Carter knew he would never shed. "I tried, but Isabel clung to my hand, pleading with me not to leave her. I think she knew," he said, his words choked. "And she didn't want you to see how broken she was. Her last thoughts were of you and Katie."

Nathan turned to look at him, his eyes glistening, his cheeks, as expected, tearless.

"She asked me to keep you and Katie safe and happy for her," Carter said, lowering his gaze to the table. "I've done my best to hold to that promise. I only wish I could have done more."

"More?" Nathan countered, his tone tight with emotion. "You were there to comfort Isabel in her final moments, protecting her from the cold and the rain, your promise giving her the peace she so desperately needed before she was taken from this earth." He crossed the room to clasp a firm hand over his brother's shoulder. "To know that Isabel didn't take her last breath frightened and alone, that she was with someone who loved her, eases some of the guilt at not having been there for her when the storm hit."

"Audra said your knowing the truth would give you comfort, but I wasn't so sure."

"Audra knows?" Nathan replied, his words gravelly.

"We talked after we left your place following the pizza party. I needed her to understand."

"Understand why you were so intent on pushing her in my direction?"

Carter frowned. "You and Audra deserve to be happy again and the two of you are both raising children alone. It seemed like the right thing to do at the time."

Nathan raised a dark brow.

"I gave my word to Isabel…"

"If Isabel were here," his brother said, shaking his head, "she'd call you a misguided fool. Sure, Audra and I have children we're raising by ourselves, but her heart is all yours."

A small smile tugged at the corners of Carter's lips. Isabel had called his older brother a misguided fool a few times during their courtship and she'd been spot-on. "Reckon Isabel would have the right of it in calling me a misguided fool. We Coopers seem to have a knack for taking a few wrong roads before finding the right one. But I had to try. Yours and Katie's happiness means the world to me. I'd gladly sacrifice my own to give that back to you."

"Carter," his brother said, his expression serious, "I'll never forget what you did for Isabel, or the selflessness you've shown when it comes to seeing that Katie and I are happy. But I'm asking you to let it go as far as my happiness is concerned. I buried my heart with my wife the day we laid her to rest. There will never be anyone else for me."

He wanted more for his brother, but he had to honor his brother's wishes. Carter nodded, accepting that he couldn't make Nathan love again. "I've got to admit it would've been a hard pill to swallow, having to step aside while you became the man Audra and the kids counted on." Carter stood. "Speaking of which, I'm hoping she'll agree to count on me for the rest of her life."

Nathan's eyes widened. "You're gonna ask her to marry you?"

"It's the right road to take," he said with a grin.

"You've only known her for a few months," he reminded him, sounding like the big brother he was.

"Maybe so. But I feel like I've been waiting for her for all of my life."

* * *

Audra reached for the remaining flower pack in the flat she'd picked up at Hope's Garden that afternoon on the way home from church. She'd needed a few more than she'd purchased with Carter the weekend before, but she also needed something to busy her thoughts with so they didn't stray to all the reasons why Carter hadn't asked to come by after church as he always did. Sure he'd sat with her and the kids, but there had been something weighing on his mind. Maybe he and Nathan had some issues to work through on their plans for the rec center that couldn't be done during the week because of other jobs they were trying to finish up. Or maybe he was regretting having asked for more where their relationship was concerned. Or maybe…

Her troubled thoughts drifted off at the sound of a truck coming up the drive. Glancing back over her shoulder, Audra's heart leaped as Carter pulled up to the house. Grabbing onto the newly painted porch rails, she pulled herself to her feet and peeled off her gardening gloves, dropping them onto the deep, rich earth below. Then she turned and stepped from the colorful flower bed with a welcoming smile.

He stepped down from the pickup and met her gaze with a tempered smile.

Oh, how she'd missed spending time with him, even if most of that time had been spent with the two of them working together on house renovations. The children had missed him, too, constantly asking her when he would be coming by. That past week Carter had been overwhelmed at work, between finishing up current jobs and preparing for the start of the rec center. And while she understood, that didn't keep her from missing the time they'd shared together.

He walked toward her in long, determined strides, his gaze intense and locked firmly with hers.

Before she could utter his name, he swept her up into his arms and held her tight. "Darlin'." He sighed into her hair, sounding almost vulnerable.

"Carter," she said worriedly, "is everything all right?"

"Because of you," he said, "it's gonna be." He lowered her feet back to the ground, his arms still locked about her waist as he looked down at her with eyes filled with emotion. "I just came from talking to Nathan," he said, reaching up to brush a stray strand of hair away from her face. "He knows about Isabel."

"Oh, Carter," she groaned, knowing how hard this must have been for him. She herself had been putting off calling Bradford because to do so would stir up painful memories.

"I'm okay, darlin'," he said. "It's what needed to be done. You gave me the strength to see it through. And Nathan is gonna be okay, too. You were right. He was grateful that I was there to comfort Isabel during her final moments."

She caught his face between her hands and looked up at him lovingly. "I'm so proud of you."

"I can't believe I almost gave you away to my brother," he said regretfully. "You and the kids mean the world to me. That day I saw you dangling from that rickety old front porch, my life changed. You made me feel again. You made me rethink my plan to remain single, to keep my heart safe. You made me feel a part of your beautiful family. Made me want your family to be mine forever."

Her hand flew to her mouth, smothering a gasp.

"Darlin'," he said with a gentle smile, "I'm finally at a point where I can move on. I've forgiven myself for holding the truth back from my brother and he's forgiven me for keeping it from him. I'm ready to put my heart on the line where you and I are concerned. I—"

"Hold that thought," she said, placing a finger to his lips.

He arched a questioning brow. "Audra?" he mumbled against the press of her finger.

"Before you say anything, I need to do some forgiving myself," she told him. "Please, come inside and give me strength while I make a call I've been trying to gather the courage to make."

"Where are the kids?" he asked as they stepped up onto the porch.

"Out back kicking balls around so Boone can chase after them," she said as she drew open the screen door. "Those three have become inseparable."

He followed her back to the kitchen, where a light summer breeze drifted in through the open window over the sink. "This won't take long," she told him as she reached for the cell phone she'd left lying on the kitchen counter.

Nodding, he settled onto a chair at the table to wait.

With trembling fingers, Audra punched in a number she hadn't used in what felt like forever. One she'd deleted from her contact list the day Bradford legally gave up any and all parental rights. Then she waited, her anxiety growing with every unanswered ring on the other end of the line. She needed to do this so both she and Carter would be free to move on. "Please pick up," she muttered in frustration.

A hand captured her free hand, long, strong

fingers weaving their way through hers. And in that single gesture, her trepidation faded.

The ringing ceased, followed soon after by a voice. "Bradford Marshall speaking."

Audra tensed at the sound of her ex-husband's voice, her grip tightening around the phone.

"Hello?" he said, sounding annoyed by the pause in response.

"Bradford, it's Audra."

"Audra," he said, his tone instantly changing, much to her surprise. "How are you?"

"I'm doing well."

"Glad to hear it."

No "how are the kids?" she wanted to say, but this call was about forgiveness and moving on. Not rehashing old hurts. "The kids are doing well, too. We're settling in and the kids are very happy here."

"In that tiny little Texas town?"

Audra's eyes widened at the unexpected question. "How do you know where we are?"

"I got your forwarding address from the post office. I was going to come down there."

"Why?" she said, her panicked gaze shooting up to meet Carter's calming one. She wanted to feel that same sense of calm, too. But what if Bradford intended to try and get custody back?

Was it even possible at this point? If so, she'd fight it with everything she had in her.

"Because things are different now," he replied. "I've changed. I'd like for us to give our marriage a second chance. For the children's sake."

A second chance? Had he lost his mind completely? "They're not *your* children," she reminded him. "Not anymore. You chose to give them up."

Carter gave her hand a gentle squeeze, reminding her that he was there for her.

"I wasn't thinking straight at the time because of the alcohol," he said, as if that were a reasonable defense for abandoning his children.

Excuses. Bradford was good at that. His drinking and affairs started long after his emotional neglect of his children. "None of that matters now. I'm calling to tell you that I forgive you for the wrongs you've done to us. It's time for me to move on with my life. To relish in a happiness that I was never able to have with you."

"You've met someone?" he said, as if the idea of her finding someone else was completely preposterous.

Her gaze locked with Carter's. "I've more than met someone," she said with a tender smile. "I've found someone who likes me just the way I am."

"Loves you," Carter amended, not bothering to keep his voice low.

Audra's focus was no longer on the call she'd made, but on the man standing next to her. "You love me?" she said in a surprised whisper.

"Mommy!" Her son's terrified scream filtered in through the open window.

Audra's head snapped around, her gaze searching the yard outside. She'd never heard Mason sound so panicked. In the distance, she heard Boone's frantic barking. So many things went through her mind all at once. None of them good.

"Lily!" her son's wail from somewhere beyond the pines had all the breath leaving her lungs.

Audra felt as though her legs were going to buckle beneath her. "Something's happened to Lily," she gasped.

Carter was out the door in an instant.

"Audra?" her ex-husband said on the other end of the line.

"I have to go."

Audra raced after Carter, whose long legs already had him disappearing into the small cluster of pines that grew in her backyard. Her heart was pounding and she still had the phone clutched in her hand.

"Where is she?" she heard Carter demand from somewhere near the pond.

She broke through the trees to see her wild-eyed son looking up at Carter, his face as white as a ghost.

"In the pond," he sobbed, pointing toward the small body of water with its long-stemmed cattails and vibrant yellow patches of water lilies. "I only left her for a minute. When I came back she was paddling real hard. I thought she was coming out, but then she just stopped."

Carter didn't wait for Mason to finish his explanation of what had happened. He shot past her son, charging into the water.

"No," Audra said in a low, keening moan. Not her baby girl. *Dear God Almighty, please don't take my baby from me.* A few feet away from the grassy bank, the red ball her daughter had been kicking around the yard all afternoon bobbed up and down atop a cluster of bright yellow water lilies. Her gaze moved ahead of Carter, searching frantically for her daughter. And then she saw her. Facedown, long, golden brown hair fanning out around her. Boone was in the water with her, paddling around her.

Then Carter was there, reaching past the pup for her daughter, his deep voice calling out

Lily's name as he turned her over. He checked to see if she was breathing, his tormented expression telling Audra that she wasn't. She watched, as if through a fog, Carter carrying her daughter out of the water. As he lowered Lily's pale, lifeless body to the deep green grass below, Audra prayed harder than she had ever prayed in her life.

"Call 911!" Carter shouted out as he bent over Lily to begin the CPR he'd been trained to do years before as a volunteer firefighter. *Please God, let her live.* Because at that moment there was no life in her tiny body.

Boone had followed them out onto the bank and was now pacing around them in worried whimpers. Carter began counting compressions. Behind him, Audra choked out her plea for help to the 911 operator. Mason stood a good distance away, sobbing loudly. At the end of the compressions, he gave two rescue breaths.

Breathe, baby girl, breathe, he thought in desperation as he paused to see if she'd begun to breathe on her own yet. She hadn't.

"Carter," Audra pleaded as she sank onto her knees beside him.

He recalled the words she'd spoken that day he'd offered to teach her children to swim once the water warmed. *I trust you to keep my children safe.* Why hadn't he made the time to teach them sooner? Learning to swim in cold water was better than this. He began compressions again, silently praying for God's good grace.

Suddenly, Lily coughed and sputtered. Carter tipped her head to the side as water spilled from her blue-tinged lips. While she wasn't completely out of danger yet, she had a pulse and was breathing once more. Closing his eyes, he sent up a prayer of heartfelt thanks to the good Lord for giving Lily back to them.

The second Carter stepped into the hospital room, Audra was in his arms, clinging to him like a lifeline. He ran a hand up and down her back, holding her tight as she sobbed against him. Then he saw the empty hospital bed and his heart dropped. "Lily?" he said, forcing the word out.

"They took her for some tests."

Relief like he never knew it spread through him. "How is she?"

"Alive," she said, looking up at him with her tear-streaked face. "Because of you."

Tears bit at the backs of his eyes as he struggled to remain strong for her. "I love her," he admitted. "Like she was my own flesh and blood. And I would do anything within my power to keep her safe."

She nodded. "How is Mason?" she asked worriedly.

"All settled in at Millie's," he replied with a tender smile. "She'll see to it he has all the coddling he needs while you're here."

"Thank you." She bit at her bottom lip. "I'm worried about him. I know he blames himself for not being able to save Lily."

"We had a man-to-man talk about that on our way to Millie's. He understands now that accidents happen and that his sister is alive today because of his getting her help so quickly. He's gonna be just fine."

"Thank you for that."

He nodded. "Will you be okay if I step out of the room to call my brothers? They'll be wanting to know how Lily is."

"You don't have to stay at the hospital," she said, biting at her bottom lip as if holding back a plea for him to do otherwise.

"Darlin', I wouldn't be anywhere else. My place is right here by your side. And I'm not leaving until Lily can come home with us, however long it takes."

Tears spilled down her cheeks. "You are so good to my children."

Reaching up, he brushed a tear away from

her damp cheek. "I'm really hoping they can be my children, too, someday very soon. But we'll have plenty of time to sort things out once we get Lily home. For now our focus needs to be on her and her alone."

She nodded in agreement. "I used to pray Bradford would come to his senses and realize what it was he was giving up, but his actions led me to you." She looked up into his eyes, a smile lifting the corners of her mouth. "And I couldn't love you more if I wanted to."

His heart swelled with her admission. "That goes both ways, darlin'." His daddy's words came back to him in that moment. *There's always hope beyond the storm.* His daddy had been right. Lowering his head, he brushed a sweet kiss over her lips. "You are my heart. That's why loving you comes so easily. And together we're gonna weather this storm and find that big, bright rainbow on the other side."

"Go call your brothers," she said, giving him a gentle shove, "before you have me bawling my eyes out all over again."

"Can't have that now, can we?" he said with a teasing smile. "I won't be long."

Carter made his way to the family waiting room, which was, at that moment, currently empty. He needed a moment alone. Needed to take a second to breathe now that he knew Lily was in good hands. Knew he needed to stay strong for Audra. But Lord help him, emotionally he was being pulled apart at the seams.

Sliding his cell phone from pocket of his still damp jeans, he frowned. He'd forgotten he'd had it with him when he'd gone into the pond after Lily. Calling his brothers would have to wait.

"Carter?"

He turned from pacing the waiting room to see his brothers standing in the open doorway. Emotion knotted up in his throat, making it hard to respond. He'd remained strong until the ambulance arrived and took Lily and Audra to the hospital. Even after he'd dropped Mason off at Millie's place on his way to the hospital. But now that the adrenaline had worn off and the reality of what had happened settled in, he was as shaky as a newborn foal.

"How's Lily?" Nathan asked as they stepped into the room, a brown paper bag clutched in one hand.

"They're monitoring her closely," he said, his words raspy. "Because of the water she had in her lungs, she's at risk for pneumonia. They also need to see if there was any neurological damage done as a result of her…" The remainder of his words caught in his throat as the memory of Lily lying before him, lifeless, played through his mind.

Nathan stepped into the small family waiting area with Logan right on his heels, pulling Carter into a firm bear hug. Logan joined in, wrapping his long arms around them both.

"She's gonna be all right," Logan said with more conviction than Carter had ever heard from him before.

They stepped apart and Carter dragged the sleeve of his shirt across his damp eyes. "I know she will," he said with a nod, wanting desperately to believe it. "Because we were able to reach her immediately after it happened, thanks be to God, and to Mason, her odds of a full recovery are much better."

"And to you," Nathan reminded him. "I understand you had to do CPR on Lily."

Carter nodded. "I've never been so scared in my life," he admitted without shame. "It's been years since I've had to perform CPR and that had only been on a dummy. I was afraid I might not remember what to do and the life of Audra's little girl depended on my putting what I'd been trained to do back then into action. I knew I couldn't let her down."

"And you didn't," Logan said with an empathetic smile. "Audra has her little girl."

Carter had to take a seat, settling himself into

one of the beige, modular chairs that lined the waiting room wall. "She's gonna be my little girl, too," he said as he sat back, dragging a hand down over his face. He looked up at his brothers, who were staring at him as if trying to process how he would manage that. Taking pity on them, he said, "When we get Lily home safe and sound, I'm gonna ask Audra to marry me. And, if she'll allow it, I'm gonna legally adopt Mason and Lily and be the daddy they both deserve."

"Just when I was considering asking Audra to marry me," Logan said with a playful sigh.

"Gonna have to get in line behind me," Nathan added.

Carter knew better. Marriage anytime in the near future was the furthest thing from Nathan's mind. And with all his talk about this female and that, Carter knew his younger brother was still hung up on his first love. But their teasing jests helped to ease some of the emotional tension gnarled up inside him. "I know Momma raised us boys to share, but that's not happening in this case. You're gonna have to go find your own women to propose to."

"But you're getting yourself a package deal," Logan protested. "A sweet, beautiful wife and a couple of really great kids all in one shot."

"That I am," Carter answered with a widening grin.

Nathan placed the bag he had in his hand onto a nearby table. "You'd best make use of these if you wanna keep Audra thinking fond thoughts of you."

He looked to the bag. "What is it?"

"A change of clothes. Figured you could use it."

"No doubt about it now," Logan said, screwing up his face. "He smells like he bathed in a mixture of fish and muck."

"I do?" Carter said, frowning as he looked down at his sodden clothes. And to think he'd been holding Audra in his arms smelling that way.

Nathan chuckled. "He's only yanking on your reins. You don't smell *that* bad."

He certainly hoped not. Smelling like pond muck and fish was not the way to make a woman want to spend the rest of her life with you. And that's exactly what he intended to do.

Chapter Twelve

With Lily home recovering from what could have been a tragic accident, Audra's thoughts turn to the man who had saved her daughter's life and the words he'd spoken to her at the hospital. *I'm really hoping they can be my children, too, someday very soon.* Another man's children, yet Carter loved them, protected them, as if they were his very own. He loved her.

Yet, she couldn't forget that she had trusted in love once and it had gone so terribly wrong. Her choices had caused her children emotional pain. But Carter wasn't Bradford. Not even close. He would never abandon her or her children. She believed that wholeheartedly. And, more importantly, she trusted him. Not only with their lives, but also with her carefully guarded heart.

True to his word, Carter had been at that hospital every single evening of Lily's stay, even after that stay had been extended by the onset of pneumonia. She was certain he would have been there more, but Audra had insisted he not miss any work, that she and Lily would be fine. After a good amount of grumbling, he finally conceded.

Millie, bless her dear, giving heart, didn't just offer to keep Mason for her, seeing him off to school each day, but Boone, as well. It worked out well, because Katie came there every day after school and stayed until Nathan finished working and came to pick her up. Carter did the same with Mason, picking him up after work and bringing him in to the hospital to spend time with Audra and Lily, sometimes with a carryout from Big Dog's to give her and Lily a break from hospital food. Then he'd take her son back to Millie's to get ready for bed and he'd return to the hospital to sit with her and Lily couple more hours before finally going home. Even when her daughter's stay ended up lasting longer than expected as Lily came down with pneumonia, Carter was there for her.

She'd gone from seeing him every day during Lily's recovery to only two times that past week as he and Nathan were in the opening phase of construction on the rec center. And oh, how she missed him. Did he feel the same?

Or had everything they'd gone through with Lily had him rethinking what it was he really wanted?

Audra pushed those niggling doubts away. If she didn't have faith in what she and Carter had together, then she didn't deserve him. But she did long to see him. Maybe, just maybe…

Pulling her phone from her purse, she dialed Carter's cell and waited to leave him a message, asking him to call her back whenever he had time. Only, much to her surprise, he answered her call.

"Afternoon, darlin'," he drawled.

His greeting brought a smile to her face. She had become quite fond of hearing him call her that. Even if *darlin'* was quite commonplace in Texas. There was still a world of difference in hearing Carter call her that as opposed to the butcher in the grocery store.

"I'm sorry to bother you while you're at work."

"No bother," he said. "As a matter of fact, you can call me anytime it suits you. I like hearing that sweet voice of yours. Everything okay?"

"Yes," she said, blushing. "Everything's fine. I was just wondering if you might be free for dinner tonight. If not, it's okay. I know you and Nathan have been putting in some long hours this week."

"We have, but a man needs a good home-cooked meal every once in a while. Dinner sounds great. I was gonna stop by this evening anyhow. Been missing you like crazy, darlin'."

"Same here," she said softly.

"I have a few ends I need to tie up before I can get there. Does six work for you?"

"Six is perfect. I'll see you this evening."

Carter made his way up to Audra's house, a large bouquet of red roses in one hand, a smaller version of them in the other. He'd no sooner stepped up onto the porch when the screen door flew open and Mason, Lily and Boone raced outside to greet him.

Kneeling, he accepted their welcoming hugs as well as a couple of wet puppy kisses to his cheek. Holding the smaller bouquet out to Lily, he said, "These are for you. They're get-well-soon flowers."

She smiled and brought them to her nose, giving them a big sniff. "They smell good. And they're pretty, too."

"Pretty girls should have pretty flowers." He glanced around. "Speaking of which, where can I find your momma?"

"You can find her right here," Audra called out to him from the other side of the screen door. Pushing it open, she said, "Mason, why don't you go help your sister find a vase to put her flowers in? I think there might be a couple under the kitchen sink."

"Okay." He turned to Lily. "Come on."

Lily followed, admiring her fragrant bouquet as she went. Boone trailed behind them, tail wagging happily.

"That was sweet of you," Audra said.

"Yep, that's me," he said with a teasing grin. "Sweet yet manly cowboy."

She laughed as she held the door open for him. "I'm so glad you could make it tonight."

So was he. Straightening, Carter moved toward her, feeling like a man who'd been lost in the desert and had just found himself a cool drink of water. The second he stepped foot inside the house, Audra threw her arms around his neck in a welcoming hug. "I've missed you."

"Darlin'," he murmured, returning her embrace. When the hug ended, he chuckled. "Now that's the kind of greeting a man could get used to after a long day's work."

"I'll have to keep that in mind," she said with a smile.

"These are for you," he said, pulling the much larger bouquet of red roses from behind his back. Flowers that he'd had bound with a delicate lace ribbon. "I have it on good authority that red's your favorite color."

"It is," she said, her smile widening. "Carter, they're beautiful!"

"No, you're beautiful."

"A girl could get used to such lovely flattery."

He chuckled. "I'll keep that in mind. What do you think of the ribbon I chose?" he said, nodding toward the bouquet. "I picked it out special just for you."

He watched as her gaze dropped to the delicate lace fixings at the base of the flowers. The moment he knew she'd seen the gold band with its single solitaire diamond tied to the bouquet with a strip of that same delicate lace ribbon, he dropped down onto one knee.

"Carter," she gasped as he reached out to untie the ring from the lace, holding it up to her.

"I know we haven't known each other all that long, but I've come to love you. I find myself counting the hours until I get to see you again and then resent how quickly time passes whenever I'm with you. I wanna be able to spend each and every day with you and your children and that overzealous pup of theirs. Audra Marshall," he said, reaching for her hand, "will you do me the honor of becoming my wife?"

Before she could answer, a car pulled up the drive, drawing their gazes that way. "Oh, no," she gasped as the car came to a stop in front of the house.

"Darlin'?"

"It's Bradford."

He shot to his feet, his brows furrowed into a frown. "Your ex-husband?"

"Yes."

"What does he want?"

She shrugged, biting at her bottom lip. "I don't know."

They watched as Bradford stepped out of a sleek, red sports car and walked with an over-inflated confidence to the porch.

Audra reached for the door.

"I'm going out there with you," Carter muttered unhappily.

"I'd rather you didn't," she said, placing a hand on his arm. "This is something I need to do on my own."

"I don't like it."

She rose up to brush a kiss over his lips. "Trust me, Carter. Please."

He gave a reluctant nod, wanting to respect her request, but it wasn't easy. So he waited there in the entryway while the woman he loved went outside to talk to the man she'd once been married to.

"Hello, Audra," he heard the man say.

"What are you doing here, Bradford?" she replied, lacking her usually welcoming tone.

"I came to check on my daughter."

"We've been over this before. She's not *yours* any longer. Lily nearly died almost a week ago. You knew that because I left you a message telling you so. I should've learned my lesson the first time when our daughter nearly died from that burst appendix and you couldn't spare her a minute of your time."

Carter pressed a hand to the wall and hung his head, fighting back the rage at hearing what Bradford had done. Or not done, as was the case. Lily could have died. How could the man not have been there when his daughter needed him the most?

"I had no choice. I had to work to keep a roof over our heads back then," he heard Bradford reply. "But I've moved up at the firm and have the ability to rearrange my schedule, if need be. I did just that so I could fly down here and be with you and our children during Lily's medical crisis."

"A week after the fact," she said coolly. "Nothing's changed."

"I know you're angry with me, Audra, but you have to believe me when I tell you I have changed. It took your walking out of my life to realize what I'd lost. I've cut back on the time I spend working. I even stopped drinking for you."

"You stopped drinking *for me*?" she repeated.

Carter couldn't get a read on her feelings at that moment. Audra had been so torn over breaking her wedding vows and divorcing Bradford. Would guilt, maybe even some deeply buried feelings, carry her back to him if he truly were a changed man? His fingers moved over the diamond ring he had clutched in his hand.

"I'm ready for us to be a real family," her ex went on. "You and I both know it's what God would want."

Carter's jaw clenched. The man was using her faith to try and influence Audra's decision. If he stood there any longer, he wouldn't be able to keep from giving in to the urge to step outside with Audra and wrap a possessive arm around her waist to let her ex know her heart was no longer his. It belonged to Carter.

But it didn't. Not completely. Audra had yet to accept or reject his proposal of marriage. Turning away from the door, he strode through the house and past the kids, who were busy filling up a vase with water in the kitchen. Slipping out the back door and down onto the patio, Carter dragged in a deep, calming breath.

Trust me, Carter.

After long moments of pacing, he stopped and lifted his face to the sky. "Lord, give me the strength to let her go if that's what Audra chooses."

"Audra chooses you."

His head snapped around to find her standing there on the porch, a deep tenderness in her pretty amber eyes.

"And Bradford?"

She smiled. "Is on his way back to Chicago." She stepped down from the porch, moving toward him. "I never truly knew what love was until I met you. Bradford will always be a part of my past, but you, Carter Cooper, are my future. So in answer to your earlier question, yes, I would love nothing more than to be your wife."

"Darlin'," he said as he drew her into his loving arms, "I want the whole package, as my brothers would say. You and the kids. How would you feel about my legally adopting Mason and Lily and giving them my last name?"

"Oh, Carter," she said, thick tears springing to her eyes.

"Am I gonna have to fetch a bucket?" he teased with a loving grin.

"Most definitely."

Epilogue

"You may kiss the bride," Reverend Johns announced as he closed the bible he held in his hands.

A slow grin hitched up one side of Carter Cooper's mouth as he drew his new wife into his arms. "I do," he told her in a slow drawl.

Audra giggled softly. "I think that part's over."

"Can't seem to keep from saying it," he replied. "Because, darlin', *I do* love you. *I do* thank the Lord for bringing you into my life. And *I do* like your pecan pie."

"Carter," she said with an impatient sigh.

Carter grinned as he dipped her back over the crook of his arm and kissed her, his heart overflowing with the love he felt for her.

Clapping arose from the small gathering of family and friends that had come to Braxton's only church that afternoon to witness his and Audra's marriage.

As Audra straightened, her cheeks holding a soft blush, Carter turned to his best man and held out his hand for a man to man shake. "You did a fine job holding on to your momma's ring for me, son."

Mason's tiny chest puffed up with the compliment and bit back a smile as he shook Carter's hand. "I wasn't going to let it roll away, 'cause then she wouldn't be able to marry you. And Lily and me want to keep you."

"That so?" Carter said with a grin.

Mason nodded.

"Well, I'm real glad you two wanna keep me. 'Cause I'm in this for the long haul." Turning, he looked past Audra to her maid of honor, who looked as pretty as a buttercup in her little yellow ruffled dress and white patent leather shoes. "And you did a fine job holding on to my ring for your momma."

"I had to," Lily said. "I'm her made-to-order."

"Maid of honor," Audra amended with a loving smile.

The reverend, who had been patiently waiting while Carter acknowledged Audra's children, children he would make his own as soon as legally possible, looked to Carter. "All set?"

Carter nodded. "All set." Reaching for Audra's hand, they turned to face those that had come to share in their joy.

"May I present, for the first time, Mr. and Mrs. Carter Cooper. May the two of you walk together in both faith and love for as long as you both shall live."

More applause filled the room as Carter reached for Audra's hand, each taking hold of their children's hands as they made their walk back down the aisle as the family they were always meant to be.

* * * * *

Dear Reader,

I hope you enjoyed *Her Texas Hero*, the first book in my Texas Sweethearts series. This series revolves around three brothers who find strength in each other and in the Lord as they overcome loss and heartache with the help of three very special women.

A big fan of HGTV, I am always watching shows on renovating houses, flipping houses, etc., and found myself thinking what if the heroine of one of my stories buys a dilapidated old house, one that's as broken down physically as she is emotionally. This became the case with my heroine, Audra Marshall. Of course, it worked out perfectly that Carter Cooper owns a construction company. I love creating a story where both the hero and heroine are broken in some way, and, in the Lord's bringing them together, find healing as well as true happiness.

I hope you'll pay a return visit to my fictional town of Braxton, Texas, this November for Nathan Cooper's story, *His Holiday Matchmaker*, where his young daughter sets out to get the one thing she truly wants for Christmas—a new mommy.

I love to hear from my readers. You can contact me via my email: katbrookes@comcast.

net or through Facebook. News and book release info can be found at my website— www.katbrookes.com.

Kat Brookes

LARGER-PRINT BOOKS!

GET 2 FREE
LARGER-PRINT NOVELS
PLUS 2 FREE
MYSTERY GIFTS

Love Inspired®

SUSPENSE
RIVETING INSPIRATIONAL ROMANCE

Larger-print novels are now available...

REQUEST YOUR FREE BOOKS!
2 FREE WHOLESOME ROMANCE NOVELS
IN LARGER PRINT
PLUS 2
FREE
MYSTERY GIFTS

✻✻✻✻✻✻✻✻✻✻✻✻✻✻✻✻✻✻✻✻✻✻✻✻

HEARTWARMING™

✻✻✻✻✻✻✻✻✻✻✻✻✻✻✻✻✻✻✻✻✻✻

Wholesome, tender romances

YES! Please send me 2 FREE Harlequin® Heartwarming Larger-Print novels and my 2 FREE mystery gifts (gifts worth about $10). After receiving them, if I don't wish to receive any more books, I can return the shipping statement marked "cancel." If I don't cancel, I will receive 4 brand-new larger-print novels every month and be billed just $5.24 per book in the U.S. or $5.99 per book in Canada. That's a savings of at least 19% off the cover price. It's quite a bargain! Shipping and handling is just 50¢ per book in the U.S. and 75¢ per book in Canada.* I understand that accepting the 2 free books and gifts places me under no obligation to buy anything. I can always return a shipment and cancel at any time. Even if I never buy another book, the two free books and gifts are mine to keep forever.

161/361 IDN GHX2

Name _____ (PLEASE PRINT)

Address _____ Apt. #

City _____ State/Prov. _____ Zip/Postal Code

Signature (if under 18, a parent or guardian must sign)

Mail to the **Reader Service:**
IN U.S.A.: P.O. Box 1867, Buffalo, NY 14240-1867
IN CANADA: P.O. Box 609, Fort Erie, Ontario L2A 5X3

* Terms and prices subject to change without notice. Prices do not include applicable taxes. Sales tax applicable in N.Y. Canadian residents will be charged applicable taxes. Offer not valid in Quebec. This offer is limited to one order per household. Not valid for current subscribers to Harlequin Heartwarming larger-print books. All orders subject to credit approval. Credit or debit balances in a customer's account(s) may be offset by any other outstanding balance owed by or to the customer. Please allow 4 to 6 weeks for delivery. Offer available while quantities last.

Your Privacy—The Reader Service is committed to protecting your privacy. Our Privacy Policy is available online at www.ReaderService.com or upon request from the Reader Service.

We make a portion of our mailing list available to reputable third parties that offer products we believe may interest you. If you prefer that we not exchange your name with third parties, or if you wish to clarify or modify your communication preferences, please visit us at www.ReaderService.com/consumerschoice or write to us at Reader Service Preference Service, P.O. Box 9062, Buffalo, NY 14240-9062. Include your complete name and address.

HW15

WESTERN WP PROMISES

YES! Please send me **The Western Promises Collection** in Larger Print. This collection begins with 3 FREE books and 2 FREE gifts (gifts valued at approx. $14.00 retail) in the first shipment, along with the other first 4 books from the collection! If I do not cancel, I will receive 8 monthly shipments until I have the entire 51-book Western Promises collection. I will receive 2 or 3 FREE books in each shipment and I will pay just $4.99 US/ $5.89 CDN for each of the other four books in each shipment, plus $2.99 for shipping and handling per shipment. *If I decide to keep the entire collection, I'll have paid for only 32 books, because 19 books are FREE! I understand that accepting the 3 free books and gifts places me under no obligation to buy anything. I can always return a shipment and cancel at any time. My free books and gifts are mine to keep no matter what I decide.

272 HCN 3070   472 HCN 3070

Name	(PLEASE PRINT)

Address	Apt. #

City	State/Prov.	Zip/Postal Code

Signature (if under 18, a parent or guardian must sign)

Mail to the **Reader Service:**

IN U.S.A.: P.O. Box 1867, Buffalo, NY 14240-1867
IN CANADA: P.O. Box 609, Fort Erie, Ontario L2A 5X3

READERSERVICE.COM

Manage your account online!

- Review your order history
- Manage your payments
- Update your address

> ### We've designed the Reader Service website just for you.

Enjoy all the features!

- Discover new series available to you, and read excerpts from any series.
- Respond to mailings and special monthly offers.
- Connect with favorite authors at the blog.
- Browse the Bonus Bucks catalog and online-only exculsives.
- Share your feedback.

Visit us at:

ReaderService.com

RS15